The Empire of Things

AND OTHER STORIES

The Empire of Things

AND OTHER STORIES

by *H. L. Mountzoures*

CHARLES SCRIBNER'S SONS
New York

To Mary Ann

Contents

The Music of the Tree

Jimmy and I had been together in a crummy bar downtown, drinking whiskey sours. It was Christmas, and we had both come home to Bayport for the holidays, I from a teaching job, my brother from the Army. He's ten years younger than I. We walked back to the house and fell in the snow in the driveway, and I had to pull his skinny frame up and haul him in. I got him into the kitchen and looked at his pink, almost beardless face, and into his big gray-green eyes. Staring at him I could see Mama, but I said nothing, to avoid being maudlin. His blond hair was cropped so short that I called him Hans Hun. He let out a cowboy yelp.

Somewhere in that big, echoey tomb of a house, Father cleared his throat, and we both put our fingers to our lips and went over and shut the kitchen door so he wouldn't hear us. Neither of us would have been able to survive our big-muscled, silver-haired, iron-gray-mustached father standing there in his shorts saying, "Get the hell to bed—will there ever be peace?" My father is a strong man of noble character. He might have said, "Goddamit, no one asked either of you to come home,

Christmas or not. Go back to California, you, Professor. And you, go back to the Army. They may teach you some manners and some dignity."

Jim and I devoured salami sandwiches and were about to go to bed when Jim's girl came to the front door. Two o'clock in the morning. She is so weird—blonder than he is, with a large head and good lips, but there is fear in her almond eyes. She trembles and quivers, and she is aesthetic. She has the best body I ever saw on an eighteen-year-old girl. Her name is Sylvia. She said, "David, I'm sorry to bother you. I want to see your brother."

I went to the kitchen and told him. He grinned. "Again?" He put on his ski parka and said, "I'll be right back."

I fell asleep on the couch with the lights on, and when I woke up they were all off. I thought I dreamed of a giant in underwear shutting off the lamp at my feet and saying, "Bums. I raised two drinking bums. Look at you—thirty-three years old, with your shoes on the couch." He curled his lip back just before the relief of total darkness.

What startled me into wakefulness was Jim stumbling in. I jumped up to turn on the lamp, nearly toppling the huge Christmas tree that he and I had struggled to put up that morning. Steadying it, I grappled with its fat, furry branches. The needles pricked me, and the tree made a noise like music—scores of bulbs and ornaments clinking together, a hushed tinkling in the dark. When the tree had stopped shuddering, I put my fingers to my nostrils and inhaled the gummy, sticky smell of a Christmas tree—resin and tangerine. Incense. It was full of the delicately whipping memories of childhood—toys and baths and bedtime stories and laughter. I felt tears come to my eyes. There were Mama and Daddy and my two big sisters. I could have gone on like that, but I mustn't be sentimental, I told myself—why romanticize the past? It was probably just as bad as the present but had been smoothed and sweetened by the passage of time.

Jim whispered loudly, "What the hell are you doing, for Chrissakes?" We both reached for the lamp in the dark at the same time and our hands touched. We withdrew them with alacrity. Jim turned on the light. He sat across from me in Father's reading armchair, scrunched down with his chin in his neck, his nicotine-stained fingers holding his head up. His long legs were stretched out straight. "We just broke up," he said in his nasal, heavy voice.

"Again?" I said. "What about last year, when you flunked out of college and hitchhiked out to San Diego?"

"Yeah, but we really didn't break up then. It's got something to do with it, though, because I didn't care about her and went away to live with you and left her —she said so tonight. She thinks I'm rotten and mean. When she was all finished with her speech, I didn't say a word. I just got out of her precious little Porsche and slammed the door, and she drove off like a son of a bitch."

Jim stared at the tree. "Remember how it was here when Mama was alive, when there was Susie and Lisa and you, Mama and Dad? You were all a lot bigger than me, but there was fun. The train running around the tree, Mama running around in the kitchen fixing dinner. When I was little, when she wasn't a drunk. Even if he *was* a tyrant."

At first I wanted to punch him, but then I wanted to laugh at the soap opera of it all. I could almost hear the radio: Hammond-organ music, soapflake ads, noises of cozy shutting doors, footsteps, "Merry Christmas!"es, and a warm, hearty voice asking, "Will John survive the crisis of his paraplegic mother, the wealthy and landed Marcia Bradstreet, lurching in a wheelchair down the maids' stairs with the insurance man?"

Jimmy frowned and fell silent.

"What are you thinking of?" I said.

"Sylvia."

"Don't let it get you. It's only temporary. You'll be together before the cock crows thrice."

"Aw, c'mon. None of that Shakespeare jazz."

Then there were two of us frowning in silence in our living room, which might have been made of all the empty living rooms of America, of families grown and gone.

"That was terrible, last December," Jimmy said. "When I said goodbye to her before going to California. We went out to a party and got half tanked. When I took her home, we parked. You could see the ocean shivering down the end of her road. There was a moon. I told her not to worry, that I'd write. We got out and stood by the car for a long time, looking at the water down there. Everything was so black and quiet. Then she started crying. Sobbing. She was hanging on to me, her head on my shoulder. I looked up at the stars, and they were clear as ice. I could see my breath moving around her head. And I looked down and there were her tears on my black wool coat, clear and sparkly like some of the stars fell from the sky and landed there, right on my coat. I thought all the way to California, This was the benediction of our love. I should have written her that, but I couldn't. It was too corny. We went into her house. Her drunky mother was still up. She came over to us and said, 'Dahlings!' and waved her cigarette holder through the air. Then she says to me, 'Won't you have a drink?' and she looks at me, honest to God, like she's hot for me. It scared me, with her eyes slanty like Sylvia's, only worse, and I said, 'No, thanks, I have to go.' And we're standing there in the foyer. Sylvia puts her arms around me and starts sobbing again, and says, 'Goodbye, and write to me. There'll always be only just you, Jimmy.' The payoff is, her mother comes over and says to me, 'Why aren't you crying, young man? What's the matter that you never cry—don't you care? Why aren't you crying, too?' I went to give Sylvia a kiss goodbye, and it landed half on her mouth and half on her wet cheek, and I left. Outside, the air was all like— like old Mexican silver. My breath was coming out in clouds, and my heart was beating like a bastard. Everything was clear—the whole world. On the shoulder of my coat I could still see her tears. Stars."

"Shut up!" a muffled voice said. "Quiet! Animals!" There was a fist pounding on the wall.

"Better go to bed," I said. "He's getting mad."

Jimmy stood up and stretched. His mouth had melted from its usual bitter, turned-down corners to a mouth tasting the salt of tears. I looked at his eyes. They were perfectly dry. I said, "It'll be O.K."

"Will it?"

"I mean with Sylvia."

"Oh, that," he said. "Yeah. Well. Good night." He glided through the still house like an eddy of wind.

I sat for a long time looking at the Christmas tree, at the furniture that had been used for thirty years, at the melancholy chocolate walls, at the two prints I had put up when I was in college: one a Chagall rooster, the other a Dufy paddock scene. Their brightness and vigor and beauty of form and color were spectacularly depressing.

Mean and rotten. I thought about last September, just after Jimmy had been drafted. I was eating lunch in a coffee shop downtown. One of our neighbors named Dillon—a kid who, while growing up with him, was

Jimmy's "best buddy to the death"—came in and sat next to me. I had the pre-school-week teacher's blues. When Dillon started talking about how it was too bad Jim couldn't settle down and finish college, I said, "Don't talk to me about that kid."

"Why, what's wrong with him?"

"He doesn't care about anybody but himself. He went off and left all kinds of long-distance-telephone and dry-cleaner and car bills for my father, and he's got about three girls breaking their hearts over him, and he doesn't give a damn about a thing. He's insensitive, that's what."

"He is like hell," Dillon said. He was all freckles, a lot of teeth, big black eyes, and an intensity that was overpowering.

"What do *you* know?" I said.

"More than you ever did about him, that's for sure."

I didn't answer.

"He's cool," Dillon said. "Everyone knows that. You know what's eating him—what makes him like he is—as much as I do."

I should have shut up right then. I should have been mature, dignified, and got up and left. Instead, I said, "What *is* eating him?"

"Why, that time with your mother," Dillon said, with such naïveté I had to forgive him on the spot.

"What about it?"

"Don't get mad. *You* know, the day they took her away."

That August afternoon. I hadn't been there. I was twenty years old and in the Army myself at the time—four hundred miles away—but my sister Susie had written me all about it. The sun that Mama had so detested was out strong. A white ambulance from the county hospital crept into the yard. Mama didn't know. She was upstairs in a stupor in her dark room. Father was at work. Susie had had to do the whole thing—Father had washed his hands of it. The two men who came in the ambulance went up, in their white clothes. There were coaxing words, a scuffle, and screams. They carried her to the back of the ambulance tied down on a stretcher. Her blond hair was dripping off the stretcher, like honey. Her face was wet; her eyes stared madly. She moaned. In the background were Father's flowers—his gladiolas and bright-orange zinnias. She asked for some. One of the attendants grabbed a zinnia, ripped it up out of the earth, broke off the clumpy root, and placed the flower—a miniature sun—on her bosom as they slid her into the back of the ambulance and shut the doors. Lisa was married, so Susie was the only one there. She was crying and shaking. The men were telling her it would be all right, that Mama would be cured and that she would get the best of care, that she would be home and well again, not to cry—there, there. When the ambulance had left, pulled slowly out of the driveway, all the neighbors silently slipped back into their houses from their porches and steps and yards.

No mention had ever been made of Jimmy in all this silent frenzy. I had never considered him in it before, never felt his presence in it at all. I said to Dillon, "Where was Jimmy that day they took her?"

Dillon said, "Remember that shack that me and him built down in back of your house and mine in the woods—the one your father went nuts about because Jimmy took and ruined his tools in the rain? Well, I was watching with my mother from my kitchen, and just when the ambulance was pulling out of your place I saw Jimmy run out the cellar door, through your back yard, and down into the woods. He was in his red bathing suit, and I could see him through the trees, and he disappeared in the shack, and he stayed there for an hour inside that dark little shack. I kept looking out the window where my mother hangs the clothes, and he never came out for one solid hour. I never told him I saw him and I never asked him about it, but he wasn't the same afterward—he began to say things so bitter none of us guys could believe it. It wasn't when your mother died in that hospital that made Jimmy like he is."

I sat in the living room, staring, until I was alone with the insoluble Chagall and the Dufy, the brown walls, the worn furniture, the Christmas tree. Then I shut off the lamp. My eyes became used to the dark, and I sat in the room for a long time. Finally, I got up and grabbed a branch of the tree and gently shook it. The ornaments clunked. I pulled off a couple of needles, crushed them between my fingers.

I went up to Jimmy's room. Vaguely, I could see him sprawled in a tangle of bedclothes. The place smelled of sour-mash breath, cigarette butts, and perfume. I sat on the bed, listening to long, rhythmic breaths. After a few seconds, I put my fingers to his nostrils.

He struggled in his sleep, said, "Nnhnh," turned away, and was still again.

In the shadowy bathroom, I washed my hands with soap thoroughly under quiet-running cold water, then went to bed.

The Beating

O N MONDAY MORNING, the old Greek woman, Mara, and her daughter, Sophie, went to the flower shop. Sophie drove. She was forty-five, an old maid, and lived at home. She helped her heavy mother out of the car and held her arm as they crossed the street. Mara wore, as always, her faded black widow's garments. "Nick will have to tell us," she said. "Even if they are enemies. Oh, I pray to God that he's all right." She put her hands together and looked up at the gray sky. She spoke in Greek. She did not understand much English. Sophie had had to call the police for verification after a neighbor brought the newspaper clipping.

In the shop, hundreds of green plants grew in pots along one wall, and an old wood refrigerator was full of flowers. There were no customers. Mara's cousin, Nick, was fixing a basket of chrysanthemums. It looked ominous. Mara lifted her hands and said, "What happened to Stavros? Sophie just read me the paper and it said he was hurt. We went to his house right away. It was all locked up tight, no one in sight. Where is he?"

Nick looked at her for a second and then back at his work. Mara clutched Sophie's hand. Blood rushed to her head. "You must tell me," she said. "He's your *brother*. All right, so you hate each other. Everyone knows it. You work in this foolish store together for forty years and not talk one day. Over profits! Jealousies! Lies! But now you *must* tell me. He, too, is my cousin—my blood relative—as much as you are."

Nick looked up again. He was sixty and wiry, and had pale-gray eyes. His fingers twined laurel and brown ribbon and big yellow blossoms. "He was beat up," he said. He turned away.

"Tell me!" Mara said. "What is it?"

Nick's shoulders and the back of his gray head moved in little spasms.

Just then Mara felt the flowers and the greens cut into her dulled sense of smell—sweet, faintly nauseating—and her fear doubled. "Tell me at once!" she said. Her voice was shrill.

"He was beat up," Nick said. Now he was sobbing with loud noises, his whole short body shaking hard.

Mara went around the counter and put her hand on his shoulder. Ah, then, he's dead, she thought. In forty years, she had never seen or heard of any sign of love between the brothers. Their stubborn feud was a joke among all the Greeks in town. "Badly?" she said, her voice beginning to quaver.

"Badly," Nick said. He took out a handkerchief and blew his nose. His rough hands trembled.

Mara's eyes filled, and the green life of the store blurred. "Where is he?" she said.

"At my house."

"Sleeping? Resting?"

"Yes."

She blessed herself in the Orthodox way—three times, rapidly. After a moment, she said, "But who is taking care of him?" Nick's wife was dead, his two sons were grown and married. He lived alone in a big house.

Nick shrugged. He said, "I bring him a little food. He sleeps."

"We must take him to my house. Sophie goes to the office, but I'm home all day. I can cook him hot food, and if he needs anyone . . . All right?"

Nick said nothing.

"We'll go and get him right now."

Nick fluffed up the bouquet and shrugged again and said, "I don't care. Carousing all night. When will he learn?"

Leaning on Sophie, Mara left the shop. Outside, she shook her head slowly. She said, "Do you believe it? He cried."

They drove to Nick's two-story frame house. They went in through the back door. The kitchen was full of empty tin cans, a few dirty dishes. The table was stained with old coffee-cup rings. Mara walked through to the front. The rooms were musty, full of dust. The curtains were drawn, faded, and limp. The house needed a woman. But Nick was independent. He wanted no one. He was devoted to the memory of his wife.

Sophie helped her mother up the stairs. "Stavro!" Mara called. She clomped through two half-empty rooms—beds with just mattresses, blinds closed, staring icons. In the third room, the one nearest the bathroom, she found him. She put her hands on her face and said, "My Mother of God."

Stavros, a big man, was asleep on a double bed with no sheets or pillowcases. There was a rough, khaki-colored wool blanket over him, and his big horny feet were sticking out.

"Stavro!"

He opened his eyes and grunted and closed his mouth. She walked up close to him. "My God," she whispered. There was a dome of plastered bandage on his head. The swarthy skin of his face was bruised. The area around his eyes was purple, and a long stitched cut stood out over his right eyebrow.

"Yes," he said in a raw, sleepy voice. "You see?"

Mara wept, keeping the sound inside her. She held a handkerchief to her face with one hand, and with the other took the big dark hand of her cousin. She turned to Sophie and tilted her head. "All the relatives we have," she said. "Him and Nick. We grew up in the same house. We played together. The three of us as children slept together on the same bed back in the village." She bent a little toward the floor, moving her handkerchief rhythmically, fabricating the bed of straw, seeing it in the corner of a dim clay room. "Oh, God, help us."

"Why did they do it to you, Uncle?" Sophie said in awkward Greek.

"Why?" He lifted his hands weakly. "Why. Fools. Monsters. This violent hell we live in." His black eyes flashed. They were bloodshot, deeply drawn around the edges. The distortion made him look evil.

Snuffing, Mara said, "Tell us what happened. Who did this to you?"

He spoke slowly, spluttering—for his false teeth lay on the bureau. "Saturday night late, I'm coming home from the coffeehouse with Peter Cavallos. We had a few games of poker with all the fellows—you know. We're walking down the street to my car. I see these two young girls. I saw them before. They came into the shop in the afternoon and asked was I the one who had the apartment for rent? They saw it in the paper. I told them yes, the apartment downstairs from me. They wanted to see it, but not right then—maybe later that night? One of them said she was a nurse and worked late—the whore. They want to see the place now, they say. 'Now?' I say. 'Two o'clock in the morning? No, not now.' But it's the only time they can, they say. Then I look at that character, Peter. . . ."

Stavros stopped, seemed to waver for a moment. "So we said all right, get into the car." Stavros was looking away from Mara and Sophie. "We drove them to the house. My friend, poor Peter. He is seventy-five years old. And I'm sixty-eight myself, you know. . . . I should have understood the other car. I saw it pulling up around the corner." His voice rose in anger and bewilderment. "Ah, the four bloodthirsty ones, they planned the whole thing together. So I was going to show them the apartment, but one of them says to me how about a drink, maybe, first, upstairs? Well, I didn't mean any harm, believe me, I had no ideas—you know what I mean. I'm an old man. . . ." He looked away again.

Mara nodded and thought, Like a horse.

"And poor Peter, he is seventy-five years old. What can we do? Like I told the police, what can two old men do? Hah? We went up, and no sooner did the girls take off their coats we hear someone running up the stairs. The door opens, and there are two tall young men coming at us—one skinny, the other strong. They rush into the kitchen where we're sitting at the table, and before I know what's happening I'm standing holding up my arm and this strong one is beating me over the head with an iron. And Peter is yelling, and they are beating him with an iron, too, irons for fixing cars—flat tires— you know. If I didn't hold up my arm, he would have broken my skull."

Stavros showed them his arm; it was black, red, and blue with bruises. There were two Mercurochromed dents on his forearm—the deep marks of the round tire iron. Mara hissed air in through her gums. Sophie looked away at the wall.

"Yes, I'd be dead for sure. No doubt about it.

Poor Peter, he fell right away, and while this other monster was clubbing me, the girls were going through the drawers—the other son of a bitch, too, the skinny one. We were hollering in the beginning, but who could hear us, all the windows closed, the apartment downstairs empty? Then I was lying on the floor. They went through my pockets and took money—what, fifty, sixty dollars—the lousy crooks. If I were younger . . . But there were two of them. With irons. On helpless old men.

"They left, and we were lying there bleeding. I couldn't get up. I had no strength. I called to Peter. He didn't answer. He was bleeding, too. I thought we would lie there and die slowly. Like goats at slaughter. Who would hear us? Jesus.

"Then I heard the girls' voices coming up the stairs, and men's voices, and I prayed to God for the first time in years. I thought, They've come back to finish us off, to kill us once and for all. They came in. I could hardly see. My eye. Everything is blurred, the room is all red. . . .

"But it's just the one girl, and she has two policemen with her. They bend down to me. 'Help us,' I can just about say to them in English. 'Don't let this woman out from here,' I say. Ah, the dope. Thank God she was so stupid. She went to the police station and said there had been a bad fight between the two old Greeks in this house where she was with her boyfriend, and she had left her coat up there. She wanted her coat. Would they go with her to get it? Because she was afraid we might hurt her. Can you imagine?

"But the police figured something was wrong— there was more to it than what she said, with all the blood. Because more than half an hour had passed. There was a lake of blood on the kitchen floor, and it was splattered over the walls. God, I wouldn't be here if it wasn't for this girl. Maybe she was afraid the men had killed us. Maybe she took pity. Who knows.

"The police took us to the hospital. Peter's still there. He has a broken wrist and a concussion. But he's going to be all right, the police told me. They gave him a transfusion at the hospital. The police got the other three, the two monsters and the girl—all four of them are in jail. The girl who came for the coat told everything. The police waited for me at the hospital and took me to the station. They brought them in, and seven o'clock in the morning I identified them. 'Yes,' I said, 'that's the ones. The murderers.'

"Why? Why to old men? For fifty dollars? With irons. The police took pictures of me. Nick came and got me. He brought me here to this room, and I saw in the mirror that I should be dead. The bandage *soaked* with blood, and blood caked in my ears. I didn't recognize myself. And he washed me. The doctor put a new bandage on today, a little while ago. Nick—he washed me." Stavros stopped talking, and swallowed, and looked at his feet.

Mara was nervously wiping her nose. Sophie had stepped out into the hall. "There," Mara said. "Poor man. It's all over now. We've come to take you to my place. The couch opens into a bed. I can look after you. You'll have hot, fresh food. Soup. And clean bedclothes, and we'll get you some pajamas."

Stavros said slowly, "I guess that's a good idea. Someone to talk with. I can't go home yet. The blood."

"Come, then," Mara said, "don't think about it. I'll go and clean it." She saw the fear of death in his eyes. She said, "Can you move? Are your legs strong enough? You think you can get down the stairs? Do you have your clothes?"

"My legs are all right. Go out for a minute. Let me put on my pants."

She went out and stood with Sophie. He lumbered into the hall. The two women struggled helping him down the stairs.

They left the gloomy house. They eased Stavros into the back seat of the car, and drove a dozen blocks to Mara's bungalow. It was on a quiet street of small, similar houses and lawns with maple trees.

Mara kept saying, "I thought you were dead. Dear God. I really thought you were dead."

Finally, Stavros said, "Bah! I want to live. You in your black—waiting so patiently, so hopefully for death."

Behind the wheel, Sophie smiled faintly. Then she looked at her mother and sobered.

"No, no," Mara said. "That's the damage in your head talking, not you. I didn't mean that at all. It's not true. How could it be? You're wrong. No." She drew her shoulders together and hid in the shadows of her mind.

They came to the house, and Sophie turned off the ignition. Mara's voice was flat. She said to her cousin, "You know, when Nick told us what happened to you, he cried. He turned around behind the counter so we wouldn't see him, and he cried hard. Like a small child. Poor Nick."

Stavros sat hunched forward in his white-bandage dome. He looked at his injured arm for a long time. Then he touched one of the deep round wounds with a clumsy finger. His disfigured face contorted. He straightened up and said, "Come on. Open this goddam door and help me out."

Epithalamion

I   **M**Y WIFE IS GONE for the day. We've been married three weeks. She has soft blond hair, long, and eyes so blue they are almost purple. She just now flew over the hilltops on green transparent wings to teach her students. She'll teach them about Absolutism, the Sun King, Thomas Paine, and Karma. All on the same day. Those teen-agers' heads will split, and the radiators will hiss. My wife is wise and beautiful. When afternoon comes, she'll ride home triumphant on her silk wings, to *me*. When she folds them, I'll ask her something with my eyes. Her heart will pound. She'll flutter.

II   **H**E SITS IN THE HOUSE all day, like a long thin Buddha, and writes poems. I try to teach the children. They don't learn or care to learn. I'm too near them in age. They sit stretched, forever fondling one another in their thoughts. Adolescence, just wait! Men are frogs. We're the bugs they catch. But what am I saying! I *have* learned from him. When he looks at me with his dark eyes. I was always afraid. I cringe from pain. I think he *requires* it. He touched my hair, always gently. He said kind things, pitied me in my fatigue, my work, my new hollow life. He said that he'd take the blame. What blame? I wondered. After all, this was our arrangement, so that he might do his poems. He wor-

27

ships guilt. He eats guilt as if it were ice cream on a blazing summer afternoon. He wears it, darkly, as if it were apparel and becoming. To him, with his dark hair and olive skin, maybe it is. But *I* can't torture him. Last night, he prepared a special fish dish with all this wine and herbs and sauce, and I detested it. The tomatoes looked like clotted blood. What can I do?

III IN HER QUIET WAYS, in her long silences, she's my source of energy—my motor, my wheels, my gasoline. I can't run without her. Because she works so hard on her teaching and has little time to herself, I sometimes cook her various things. I cooked a special fish fillet last night with white wine and basil, olive oil and tomatoes. How carefully, how lovingly I prepared it. Slowly, in silence, she ate every flake. I ate fast and watched her. A compulsion seemed to be telling her, "Eat, eat it all." She filled herself; she ate so much—and she's a thin girl. I became very wise, full of the knowledge of her hating this fish.

IV HE'S SO STRANGE. After dinner, he came and touched me. I told him to go away. He went into the living room. I was preparing my lessons. I had washed the dishes, and the odor of the sad fish was nearly gone. The house was a dynamo of warmth, coziness, clickings. My pen moved. Contented, I chewed the ends of my hair as I sat at the kitchen table and made notes for tomorrow's classes. I wrote important names, dates, concepts. He came in from the living room. He walks as if he ran on wheels. He sighed, took his Loden coat from the back of his chair, and left. Immediately the house became a tinderbox. I couldn't breathe. I turned on the television set and tried to read about Louis XIV: "His height was not commensurate with his dignity, and so he wore red high-heeled shoes." A train went by, rattling the front windows. I could see its single headlight. What if he's on that train, I thought. Leaving me. Deserting a bride. But no. He came in finally, in an hour, locking the door behind him. I didn't speak to him. Why should I forgive? The gloating frog. He turned off the television. He spoke, feigning good nature. (But at least there was no liquor on his breath.) He said, "You weren't watching it anyway." I went to bed. Then I was so sorry. What had he done? Whatever he does is in my interest. I was tired. Maybe I'd been harsh. I left the light on; lying there, holding the covers, I waited, watching a spider as it clung motionless to the ceiling. The curtains were a wilderness of flowers. I walked among them. My tears fell on black tendrils, rose-and-ochre cotton petals. He didn't come. I shut off the light and fell asleep. My dreams were full of trouble—of empty fields, moving tree branches, wildly beating red visceral hearts, doors flapping and banging in the wind.

V   WHEN I CAME HOME, she looked so goddam smug. She sat there with her book, the television image sliding up and up and up. I turned off the set. She frowned. I said, as nicely as I possibly could, "You weren't watching it anyway." She got up and went to bed. I sat in the oven of a living room and considered suicide. Walks out in the country along the shore at night, moon or no moon, don't solve anything. I could use a razor blade. Or exhaust fumes from the car. Leave a note: "These are the only people I ever loved." Don't put her on the list. I heard the light in our bedroom click off. Ah, so she'd been waiting. To apportion me my permitted dollop of love. The living room was so hot I turned off all the lamps as well as the radiator valve. I dozed. Later, when I woke, I thought, I won't have myself like this. I sat up in the dark room, pulled myself up from the swamp of the studio couch. I thought, rather crookedly, Suicide is wrong. It's selfish —everyone would be vastly upset but me. I would only be dead. I went to bed. I spoke out loud to the dark, the earth, the dirt, the dust, the silence. I said, "I don't know what it was about. Or is, either. I'm sorry." She stirred next to me and drew me to her. There was no light. There was a cocoon. We crawled through, and we found the morning full of frost and sunlight, twitterings. We awoke holding each other. She said, "But now I've got to leave you and teach today. I wish it were Saturday." She put on her green coat and, carrying her black satchel of books, beautiful in the morning sun, she sailed over the housetops.

VI I WENT AROUND in the empty house kissing things: her books, her coffee cup, her makeup kit, a drinking glass, the front door. I kissed the air. I floated from one greasy dust-smeared ceiling-light globe to the next. I was a long way up. God was never higher. I came down to write poems for the day. There weren't any. No poems. Not one. Not a line, a word, a metaphor. I had shot them all. The clocks ticked wonderfully all over the house. The refrigerator hummed. I sat in shadows in complete silence the whole day, waiting for my green-winged dragonfly.

An Examination

MARK FABBRI had a three-o'clock appointment with the doctor. As he drove through the small town where he worked, where he had spent most of his life, he felt apprehensive. He parked in front of the medical center—a small professional building on a residential street. It was a raw day; the earth was hard and the trees were gray and empty. When he got out of the car, the wind flapped his coat open. Buttoning it, he went toward the building, stopped, went back to the car, and got a paper bag containing a specimen.

"I'm Mark Fabbri," he said to the middle-aged nurse in a small office just inside the door. "I have an appointment for a physical. Dr. O'Brien."

She looked at an engagement book and said, "Yes. Sit down, please, Mr. Fabbri. The Doctor will see you in a little while." Then she said, "Are you Dolores' brother?" Mark nodded. The nurse smiled and said, "You look just like her."

Mark took off his coat and hung it on a rack. He felt stupid holding the brown paper bag, and when he sat down in the waiting room he put it on the carpeting under his chair, not looking at the other people. The room was panelled and hung with watercolor scenes of sailboats.

A young technician came through a door next to the office. She said, "Miss Sampson?" and an old woman in a worn blue coat and white flat shoes got up slowly. The girl led her into a room visible from Mark's chair. "O.K., you wanna take off all your clothes and put on this gown?" she said in a surprisingly loud voice. "Dr. Turner will be in in a moment." She went out and shut the door. In a little while, she appeared in the waiting room and said, "Mr. Fabbri?" He stood up. "Come in, please," she said. He followed her. She was a bleached blonde and wore her hair in a big beehive. She looked at a manila printed form. "You're here for a physical?"

"Yes."

"Did you bring a urine specimen?"

"Oh." He pointed to the waiting room and blushed. He hurried out and brought back the bag.

"Good," the technician said. She took it. "Step in here, please." In a small room behind the office, she weighed him and measured his height: a hundred and sixty-five pounds, five feet eleven inches tall. She wrote this information on the form. Then she sat at a table and asked him questions and he answered: Thirty-two. Single. Research biologist. Connecticut Marine Laboratories. No, to a list of previous illnesses. She told him to roll up his sleeve, and she took his blood pressure. She wrote that down, too. "Follow me, please," she said. He went with her into an examining room that looked as if Mies van der Rohe had designed it, but with little glass. It contained a black leather-and-chrome table, a sink, a cabinet, and a wastebasket. Pointing to a curtained dressing booth, she said, "Take off your sweater and shirt and undershirt." She watched him. When he was stripped to the waist, she said, "You ever had an electrocardiogram?"

"No."

"O.K., you wanna come with me?" He followed

her, enjoying the languid way her hips moved as she walked before him down a long hall past closed pine doors. "Lay down on the table, please," she said when they came to the room at the end.

For a couple of months, Mark had been deathly afraid about his heart. It had taken to skipping beats, then pumping fast, causing a dizzy feeling in his head. It frightened him until he couldn't sleep at night. Finally, he decided that he must go to a doctor and have a physical examination.

The technician got the electrodes ready, rubbed gray ointment in spots on his chest, arms, and legs, and attached the suction clamps, moving them around as she progressed. They were cold. There was something clinically sexual about the whole procedure, and to ease his tension, Mark said, "Just like Sing Sing."

She smiled professionally—an old joke, no doubt. She removed the clamps and wiped his chest and arms and legs slowly with tissues. "O.K.," she said, going back with him to the first examining room. "Sit up on the table here and Dr. O'Brien will come right in." She went out swaying—bored, coldly attractive.

Dr. O'Brien did not come right in. Mark sat, chilled and sweating, for half an hour. He looked around at the grim room, and then stared out through a high, small window before him. Part of an elm showed. The thin ends of its branches swayed and bounced, first nodding Yes, and then shaking, No. Have you been growing long? Yes. Age? A hundred and five. Weight? Six tons. I seem to have trouble lifting water these days. Any history of Dutch elm disease? No, I hope not! Well, we feel that we must tell you, that you should know . . . Mark stared at the square of blue light. He had not seen many doctors in his life.

Dr. Martino was the first, when Mark was six years

33

old. It was during the Depression. Playing in the street, Mark was grazed and knocked down by a car. Someone lifted him off the cobblestones near the trolley tracks and asked him where he lived. He pointed to the brick apartment building. He was crying, not because he was hurt but because his shoe had fallen off. Someone found it and gave it to him. A mob of adults gathered. Babbling, they followed up the four flight of stairs to the apartment, where the man carrying him laid him on the sofa in the parlor. His mother became hysterical. She screamed and blessed herself, tried to get at him, and two of the women took her back to one of the dark bedrooms.

When the Doctor came, he ordered everyone out. He even told the mother to wait in the kitchen. He was a short, fat, swarthy man and had a big black mustache. A gold chain, with a small miraculous medal, hung from his vest. His shoes were scuffed, the bottoms of his pants frayed. He touched Mark's head with thick brown fingers. Then he looked inside Mark's ears, up his nose. He felt his neck and his arms, and told him to take off all his clothes.

"No." Mark began to cry.

"*Ecco, ecco,*" Dr. Martino said. He told him to stop crying and wipe his nose, that if he undressed he'd give him a nickel. Mark thought of the heavy round coin, smooth, with the picture of the animal on one side and the beautiful Indian on the other. He could hold it in his hand and keep it in bed secretly, and at last, when he wanted to, he could buy a bag of candy with it. He stripped slowly in the parlor full of antimacassars and holy pictures. The Doctor felt him all over, squeezed, tweaked, and laughed. He told the frightened mother in the kitchen that her boy was all right— nothing wrong, no damage. *Ciao!* There was no charge!

Good day! He didn't give Mark the nickel. He probably didn't have a nickel.

Then there was the dentist, Dr. Maltz, who took town welfare cases. Through the years, Mark had submitted to him like a lamb in a slaughterhouse. He was a kind man, who spoke gently—a widower. Civil, cultured, humane, he always encouraged Mark to be, too.

Mark remembered the last time he had gone for a filling, only a few months before. Dr. Maltz went at him, as usual, with genteel savagery. He cleaned his teeth, and blood poured forth as if there really were a slaughter. He drilled, pressing forward like a miner, standing firm in his thick white shoes. For Mark, dignity dissolved as he saw the Doctor's ubiquitous hairy knuckles, and his own bloody saliva dribbling uncontrollably on his yellow paper bib. Huge, ruthless eyes stared down hard on him.

In that office, too, there was a window—a constant piece of blue or gray, rain or snow-filled sky. And there were his own fingers, changing through the years from a child's to a man's, clutching the arms of the chair.

On his last visit, as always, when the ordeal was done, Mark had a feeling of relief, purgation of both body and soul, gratitude. He paid the Doctor and thanked him as he hurried toward the door. Dr. Maltz was speaking of today's wild youth, of the excellent new film of "Hamlet" playing at the Palace, of the need to work hard and to study and to enjoy all of the great opportunities in this good country as he had—he was a self-made man. The office was empty. No one was waiting. Dr. Maltz needed someone to talk to. But Mark could not bear it any longer. His penance was done. He was flushed with temporary grace, salvation. He said goodbye, closed the door with a clatter, and ran down the gloomy, varnished office-building stairs.

And, of course, there was Dr. Lawrence. Mark sat very still on the table. He looked down at the brown nipples and the black hair on his chest. In the empty room, he considered how strange and vulnerable human beings are.

Dr. Hugo Lawrence. Mark's sister Dolores had worked for him, starting when she was eighteen and Mark twenty. Dr. Lawrence was an ear, nose, and throat man. Tall and skinny, he was completely bald except for a fringe of downy blond hair. He had green eyes, a low potbelly the size of a basketball, a loping walk, a high squeaky voice, and a thin but hearty laugh. Dolores was his receptionist. They worked long hours. His waiting room was always full. Cartoons and placards hung everywhere, warning about SMOKING AND CANCER AND YOU. On one wall, mounted on pasteboard in little packs of clear cellophane, were buttons, chicken and fish bones, beads, a spool, safety pins, beans, hairpins, and a thimble—all of which children had swallowed or stuck up their noses or into their ears.

Dr. Lawrence performed surgery early in the morning, removing these objects as well as tonsils, adenoids, polyps, growths. He was silent for hours— mourned visibly—when inspections or operations disclosed cancer gone beyond hope.

He worked hard, staying in the office as long as he could. He listened without saying anything when his wife called on the telephone. Dolores told Mark that one time when Mrs. Lawrence had finished, the Doctor hung up the phone and said softly and politely, "Bitch," and went back to work pushing swabs up a patient's nose in one of the examining booths.

Dolores was very small. She had large black eyes, and a dark complexion. She was pretty and frail. She floated around and answered telephones, looked up records in files, and encouraged people in the waiting room. She was a bright ornament in the colorless routine and paraphernalia of the office. A fat nurse named Miss Lamb, with dyed black hair and gold-rimmed glasses, filled most of the Doctor's medical-work needs. Dolores was like Dr. Lawrence's child. She told him in little pieces about her home life. He was a sympathetic man. She explained that her parents had come from Italy. Her father worked for very little money trucking produce on his back in a wholesale house on River Street. His joints ached all the time. Dr. Lawrence said, "Bring him in." She did. The Doctor said, "We'll fix you right up, Mr. Fabbri." He filled him with hypodermic vitamin shots and gave him pills for his arthritic pain, free of charge. Mr. Fabbri, normally sullen and angry, thanked him meekly.

Dolores told the Doctor about her mother—that she was a crabby, lonely woman who did not know how to love anyone. She quarrelled in Italian all day with the neighbors, or sewed, or rolled out homemade pasta and cut it in thin strips, and sighed, longing for the mythical beauty of her childhood in the old country. She and her husband lived together in perpetual discord, fighting and calling each other names. "Bring her in," said the Doctor. Dolores said, "She's never left the block. Not since I can ever remember, anyway."

Finally, there was their little brother, Carl, who was then twelve—a thin fallen angel. He was alone, growing up wild. He always had a cold. "Bring him in," Dr. Lawrence said. "Are you kidding?" said Dolores. "He's so busy learning to smoke, playing hooky, fishing in back of the coal yard, and waiting till he can have a car, you'll never see *him*." And she was right. He never did.

Dolores told Mark all these things, and he began

to drop into the office—during his vacations from college, on weekends, in the early evenings to pick up Dolores to do the grocery shopping. The Doctor always asked how he felt. Mark said, "Fine." He asked what college Mark was attending. Mark told him. Muzak poured out of the walls. In the waiting room, potted plants flourished. Dolores watered them and hummed popular tunes and smiled. At home, she cried and rubbed her eyes. She was lonely.

Looking worried, Dr. Lawrence said over and over to Mark, "How are you?" Mark answered, "Fine." Then one Saturday afternoon when it was not busy, when the crowds were gone, the Doctor looked carefully into Mark's nose, ears, and throat. He said, "You have enormous adenoids. Let's get rid of them." The huge nurse, who stomped around singing and then said cruel things about patients under her breath, laid him out on a couch and stuck radium-treated wires down his nostrils. It took four appointments. The fee, Dolores told him, was sixty dollars, but the Doctor never charged him.

On several later occasions, the Doctor had him sit in one of the examining chairs. "You have a red throat," he would say. "Let me take care of it for you." Or, "You have a slight fever. A strep throat. Are you burning the midnight oil at school? Miss Lamb, give him a penicillin shot." Miss Lamb mumbled behind a curtain as she bent down and stuck the needle into him.

The months went by. Mark continued to come to the office, and Dr. Lawrence continued to say, "How are you, Mark?" It was winter, and the Doctor had usually finished a day of treating people with red eyes and noses, coughs, infected sinuses, raw throats. There were men from the boat factory, with bad ear infections from working out in the cold. Mark had come to say, "I don't feel too well. I have sort of a sore throat. My ears hurt a little." He waited. When all of the patients were gone, the Doctor put him in a booth, ran thin, stinging decongestant tubes down his nostrils, painted his throat gently, and squirted a white antibacterial powder up his nose. The Doctor performed this routine often, and then bought Dolores and Mark and himself thick hot roast-beef sandwiches at a diner on the way home. "How kind Dr. Lawrence is," Mark told Dolores afterward. "He helps Papa. You. Me. He helps everyone. He's a wonderful man." Now Mark had a father, too.

After a while, the Doctor never asked Mark any more how he felt. So Mark told him. He said, "Doctor, I have a sore throat. Not too bad, just a little scratchy." Or, "This gland hurts, kind of, right here, in my neck." Or, "My sinuses bother me, Doctor. Not right this minute, but quite often, especially in the morning." It was Christmastime, and the Muzak chimed incessant carols. Miss Lamb bounced around sterilizing instruments, changing money, giving shots, cursing faintly. Dolores picked up the constantly ringing telephones, made appointments, smiled at fragile octogenarians. (She smiled at virile young carpenters, too, and eventually married one of them.) She watered the jungle in the waiting room. The Doctor gave Mark the usual treatment and, besides, presented him with free nose sprays, throat lozenges, and antihistamine capsules. He also gave him two pound boxes of chocolates that he had got from patients as gifts. The medicine accumulated at home, unused, in a drawer. Mark's mother ate the chocolates.

One evening, Mark was in an examining booth. It was about eight o'clock. The Doctor's eyes were red and swollen, his face was pale, his shoulders drooped. Mark was telling him about his throat. The phone rang. Dolores said, "It's for you, Doctor." She covered the mouthpiece and said, "Mrs. Lawrence." The Doctor picked up the wall extension behind him. He had the big reflector on his head. "Yes?" he said. He was tired, gentle. A high-frequency noise immediately crackled on the other end. Mark heard it. It went on and on. Dr. Lawrence held the phone a little way from his ear. The Muzak was playing a love song, and the volume was amplified in the emptiness of the office, so that Mark could hear only a scattered word or phrase: ". . . cold dinners . . . sick of . . . children . . . kind of life . . ." The Doctor's face did not change. The voice was still squalling when, with dignity, he replaced the receiver softly on the hook. His face was red.

Mark said, "It's just slightly sore, on the right side. I think it's the tonsil, Doctor."

Dr. Lawrence said, "All right, let's see." He looked into Mark's mouth with his light. He took a stick cotton swab, dipped it in the usual thick amber syrup that tasted like a mixture of iodine and horehound drops. "Open," he said.

He jammed the medicine-soaked cotton into the back of Mark's throat. Furiously he pushed it from side to side, up and down, again and again. Mark grabbed the Doctor's wrist, struggled, opened his eyes wide, felt them sting with tears. The Doctor's mouth was set in a narrow, pale-pink line. Mark gagged. At last, the Doctor pulled the swab out. Mark gasped for breath, and gagged again. Tears rolled down his face. The Doctor squirted the white powder up his nose and said,"There."

Mark shook his head. The Doctor got up. He looked as if he were about to weep—as if he were sick of life and full of grief. He turned away and said to Miss Lamb, "I think that's all."

Mark held his throat, feeling the loss of Dr. Lawrence. It had been a rough way to be taught about self-pity, and anger, and the imperfections of all of our fathers. Mark stared up at the square of blue light, at the portion of elm still moving outside. He thought, Who does that leave? O'Brien himself. Mark looked at his watch. He had been sitting in here on this goddam table, half naked, for twenty minutes. Where was O'Brien?

Ah, *O'Brien,* he thought. It was a Saturday. Mark was home on leave from the Army. The family had recently moved to a cheap, two-story, frame house. His brother Carl, fifteen, was sick in bed with a temperature of a hundred and three. It was summer and Dolores immediately thought of polio. Mark arrived around eight o'clock, and found his mother mumbling and stirring a pot of lentils in the kitchen. Dolores was upstairs with Carl.

"What should we do?" she said to Mark out in the hall.

"Call the doctor, for Christ's sake. You ought to know that. Now. Who do we call?"

"O'Brien. Everyone in the office goes to him. I go to him, and he's good. Call O'Brien."

"Jesus, Dolores, why didn't *you* call him?"

"It's Papa. He says he's not paying for any doctor. He says let the welfare pay, he still has welfare rights from when he was injured with the crate of melons last month. He won't let me pay. He says he'll break all my bones if I pay."

"All right. The hell with it. Let the welfare pay, then. But call the Doctor. Suppose Carl does have polio?"

The Doctor came about eight-thirty. Dolores had said, hanging up the receiver, "He didn't sound too anxious to come. But he remembered me from the office. And I told him what we were afraid of." Dolores led the Doctor up the stairs, past her father's room, past the stale smell of his pipe and his throat-clearing noises.

Mark was standing at the head of the stairs in Carl's doorway. The sun from his mother's westerly room was streaming over him, and he felt like an absurd

41

peacetime hero in his Class-A khaki uniform, with its glittering brass, the tucked-in black tie. "Dr. O'Brien?" he said. "I'm Carl's brother, Mark. He's very sick, I think."

The Doctor nodded. He was short and stocky. He had heavy black hair, a pink face, and light-blue eyes. He looked about thirty. He examined Carl in the room with its crinkle-plastic drapes, its plywood bureau, its squeaky iron bed. The boy's clothes lay in a heap on the floor. Sports-car magazines, comic books, and dog-eared, smudged homework papers littered the bureau top, the floor. A defunct alarm clock pointed to three-thirty.

"He'll be all right," the Doctor said, coming out to the hall. "He has a virus. The flu." The Doctor's breath smelled of liquor. "I gave him a shot. Here are some penicillin pills—enough to last till Monday morning—and a prescription for more. Make him stay in bed, covered up." He turned to Dolores and said, "Force fluids." He was fastening his black bag. He looked around and seemed to be appraising the misery of the sun setting with such splendor on rough wood, linoleum, faded wallpaper, streams of floating golden dust. And there was the odor of garlic and lentils. "That'll be three dollars," he said with immense tenderness.

Mark could sense his small wiry father standing at the foot of the stairs in shadows. He could almost hear him breathing. Mark said, "Sir, this . . . this is a city case."

"Pardon?"

"Welfare." Mark felt his face flush.

The Doctor scowled. At first, he seemed to hold back some words, but then he let fly. "Listen," he said to Mark, who stood at parade rest. "I'm tired. I had a bad day. Something sad, something very unfortunate happened to a patient at the hospital today. And I told my wife I didn't want to be disturbed for anything but an emergency. We have guests. Don't you realize we're entertaining? I've got a lot of people in my yard and I have damn little time for anything. If I'd ever known . . ." He stopped. "All right," he said. "All right, I'll send you the bill. *You* have it processed and send it back to my office." He sighed and started down the dark stairs. Mr. Fabbri shuffled into his room. The Doctor disappeared around the other doorway and through the kitchen. His car started at last, and he was gone. Mark stood with his sister in the bronze and red fading sunlight and stared at the floating dust.

And that was all. All of the doctors. Until now. Mark felt like putting on his clothes and leaving. If it weren't for Dolores' swearing by him even to this day, he wouldn't have come to O'Brien in the first place.

The technician appeared with a white basket of equipment. She took Mark's right hand. She swabbed his middle finger, pricked it, and squeezed. A drop of bright blood oozed out. She collected it with a small pipette and put a fluff of cotton on his finger.

The Doctor came in, and the technician handed him the electrocardiogram. She was doing something in a corner of the room. The Doctor said, "How do you do, Mark?" Mark stood, and said, "Hi." He was surprised. The Doctor looked thin, paler than Mark remembered, and so much of his black hair had fallen out that his scalp showed uniformly through. His pale-blue eyes were clear, but there were bags under them. He wore a long white coat that made him look like a midget. A stethoscope hung from his neck; he stooped as if from its weight.

"You're here for just a physical," he said.

"Yes."

"When was the last time you had one?"

43

"When I got out of the Army."

"Oh, yes. And when was that?"

"Let's see. Eight . . . no, nine years ago."

"Why are you having one now?"

"I thought . . ." Mark looked at the technician.

"His hemoglobin is fourteen. Urine negative," she said and left the room.

The Doctor wrote it down. He picked up the ribbon of graph paper and studied the series of black, calligraphic curves. "This is excellent," he said. "Your heart is perfect."

Mark said, with relief, "To tell you the truth, that's why I came—the main reason." Then he told the Doctor about the palpitations, the skippings, the quick dizzy feeling in his head.

"Do you drink much coffee?"

"No. Two or three cups a day."

"Nerves," the Doctor said. "You don't have to worry. See?" He told him what the curves on the chart meant, the P, Q, R, S, and T curves. "See this Q curve? You have hardly any. Any at all. People with heart diseases are likely to have a big one. Or this S curve might be inverted."

Mark said, "Sometimes my ears hurt."

The Doctor checked them with his light. "They *look* fine," he said.

Over the intercom a voice said, "Dr. O'Brien, Mr. Courtenay is on Line One; do you want to talk to him?"

The Doctor paused. "All right," he said to the intercom. "Excuse me," he said to Mark. He went into the next room. The door was left open a crack. ". . . Well, listen," Dr. O'Brien said, "renew it, and have her take all of it, and if she's still vomiting tonight, call me . . . I don't care what time it is."

He came back. "Sorry," he said. Mark nodded. He

was sitting on the end of the table. "Now, about your ears," the Doctor said.

"You'll think I'm a hypochondriac or something."

"No. I want you to tell me everything. Everything."

Mark spoke in a rush, embarrassed to be complaining, wanting to get it over with. "Sometimes my ears ache. The glands in my throat hurt. They don't swell or anything. And under my arms it aches, too."

The Doctor looked thoughtful. "What else?" he said.

"In bed at night. Sometimes I feel hot and cold all over and ache. I take aspirin to stop it."

"Mmm. Anything else?"

"Well, I have trouble going to sleep."

"What do you do? I mean at your job. Your work."

"We're studying plankton—possibilities for human consumption. An algae closed-environment, oxygen-producing system for the outer-space program. Pollution—its effects on different species of local sea life."

The voice broke in again. "Excuse me, Dr. O'Brien. I'm sorry, but Mrs. Irwine is on the phone. She'd like to speak with you. Shall I have her call you back?"

Dr. O'Brien looked irritated. "No, I'll take it," he said. He smiled apologetically at Mark. "Excuse me again," he said. He went out, and this time he shut the door. Mark got up, unstuck the piece of cotton from his middle finger, and put it in the wastebasket. He sat down on the table again and folded his arms. He was sweating and felt cold. He heard the Doctor say loudly, "I said it *should have stopped* bleeding by now. I guess you'd better get him to the hospital. No, *today*. This afternoon. All right. I'll see him as soon as I can."

The Doctor came back. He shook his head. He

picked up Mark's records again. "Now. Where were we?"

"My job."

"Yes. You like it?"

"Sure. It's O.K. I've even had three papers published in the journals. But . . ."

"Yes?"

Mark shrugged. "Well, nothing . . . it's fine."

"It sounds fine. Now, let's have a look."

The Doctor examined his eyes and throat, felt his neck. He listened to his heart. He tapped his back. He told him to lie back on the table and tapped him all over, under his arms, pressed his stomach, sides, abdomen. "Good," he kept saying. "Breathe deeply. Fine." He tapped Mark's knees with a hammer and Mark's legs shot up. He tapped his ankles. The same. He put a tuning fork to his ankles. "Feel the vibration?" he said.

"Yes."

"Good."

He checked for hernia. He examined his prostate. He took him to another room and put him in front of the fluoroscope. Then the Doctor put on a long insulated apron and big insulated gloves and shut off the lights. "I can see everything," he said in the dark, mysterious room. "This is like a living X-ray. I see your heart, lungs—perfect." Mark wished that he could see, too. Would it be like underwater? Perhaps he himself could see in there what the Doctor could not—the cause of sorrow. The human condition. And what in the hell was that?

The Doctor brought him back to the examining room, and Mark sat on the end of the cold table again. "How are your feet?" the Doctor asked.

Mark laughed. "Fine," he said.

The Doctor didn't laugh. He looked as serious as if he had asked, "Your soul, Mark. How is your soul?"

"About not sleeping," Dr. O'Brien said. "Tell me about that."

"I don't get to sleep till two in the morning."

"What time do you get up?"

"Seven."

"That's not good. Why can't you sleep?"

Mark lifted his shoulders. He said, "I keep thinking in bed. I'm tired, but my mind won't stop."

"What do you think about?"

"Oh, I don't know. Everything. Everything that happened that day. Or that didn't happen. About life. I don't know." He felt inarticulate, dumb, as if his thoughts, his problems were great invisible stones on the bottom of the sea.

"Do you still live at home?"

"Yes."

The Doctor paused for what seemed an inordinately long time. "Have you tried reading?" he said.

"Sure. And then I lie awake and think about everything I've read. I reconstruct it all, the whole thing. Whether it's a novel or a lab report, the sports page, whatever."

"That's no good. No. Don't read, then. First time I ever recommended that. Well. Listen. I think that the pains and aches and the heart thing you're experiencing are from nervousness and worrying and fatigue. One thing feeds the other. But your general physical health is excellent."

Mark said, "I'm glad to hear that." Still, he felt anxious.

"Tell me," Dr. O'Brien said. "Do you have a girl?"

"There's one at the lab. And there's this teacher I take out sometimes."

The Doctor smiled. The bags under his eyes puck-

47

ered. He, too, suddenly looked vulnerable, shy. He said, "You're still young. But none of us is getting any younger. You ought to pick one out and settle down pretty soon."

Mark thought of his father, who could seldom work any more but was not quite old enough to collect Social Security, and of his mother, who had got fat and despondent.

"Now," Dr. O'Brien said, "about your fatigue and sleeplessness." He wrote on a small pad. "I'm giving you a prescription. I want you to take one of these capsules about half an hour before going to bed. This isn't a sleeping pill, it's non-habit forming, it won't give you a hangover in the morning. After you go to bed, if you're not asleep in half an hour, get up and take another one. That's all. There's no use lying there awake all night. I want you to get your rest. And let me know how everything is. Don't worry," he said. "About anything. This is a wonderful drug. I take it myself sometimes when I can't sleep. When I'm concerned about a patient. Especially a young patient with a bad heart." He shook his head slowly, as if remembering someone specific.

He tore off the prescription sheet and handed it to Mark. He said, "By the way, how's Dolores?"

"Dolores. All right, I guess." She had been married now for five years, she had borne four children, and she was falling apart.

"Such a nice girl. I saw her just a couple months back. In fact, I prescribed this very same medicine for her," the Doctor said. He looked worried. "How *is* she?" he said.

Mark raised his shoulders and dropped them. The room was silent. The elm tree outside was motionless. Mark swallowed hard.

"And the other brother. The youngster I saw once

at your house." Dr. O'Brien looked at the floor. "How's he?"

"Carl," Mark said. "He's in the Navy. He surprised us all. Turning out to be a good boy."

"Glad to hear it," the Doctor said. "Well. That's all, I guess. Good luck. I hope those pills help. They help *me*."

Mark said, "Thank you very much."

The Doctor said, "Goodbye, Mark," He walked rapidly to the door.

Mark turned and held up both of his hands. He opened his mouth. No words came. Without looking back, Dr. O'Brien went out and shut the door behind him.

Mark sat on the table looking at the hieroglyphics on the small prescription sheet in his hand. He got up. He put on his T shirt, his shirt, and his sweater, and left the room.

Walking down the hall, he heard Dr. O'Brien shouting behind a closed door, "The *pain*. Do you still feel the *pain*?" As Mark passed by, the voice of a very old man had just begun to recite a catalogue of agonies, a rosary of ancient sorrowful mysteries.

The Buoy

COSTAS AND I sat at the café on the edge of the beach at Previsa, under a pavilion of softly moving eucalypti. We were drinking FIX, the national beer of Greece. Talking in Greek, we argued, as usual, about Communism versus capitalism, but not really. We both had gone through too much for that. We were hanging the life of the heart on a quasi-political skeleton, and I think he knew it as well as I, even though he had more reason for being political than I.

"Your *freedom*," Costas said, his normally red face even redder. "Bah. You would have an empty stomach and freedom?"

"Yes," I said, "exactly."

Costas' teeth flashed, and so did his black hair and eyes, as he moved his head in mock laughter. He was handsome, intelligent, and, aside from political ideas, to me he was like a brother.

"You have never been hungry and had your so-called freedom, too, so you do not know. *I* do."

"I don't?" I said. "Are you so sure? Did you ever hear of the Depression? When I was a little boy, oh, about five years old, the same age as you were, in the late thirties, I ate bread with mustard on it, if I was lucky, but in the streets of our town I ran to my heart's content. Life was undernourished, but it was free."

"And in Athens the people were eating cats dur-

ing the war," he said. "The people were falling in the
streets from starvation by the thousands, trying to pre-
serve their freedom while the Germans held siege."

With a whisper, the long skinny leaves of the eucalypti seemed to intensify what he said.

"Why do we compare and compare?" I said, tiring.
We had been talking for a couple of hours, since noon.
"It's all the same fabric of suffering. We're just looking
at different parts of the cloth. And it's all absurd and
meaningless anyway. You said so yourself not an hour
ago. Come on. Let's go for a swim."

Costas jumped up, glad at the suggestion, and
headed toward the beach.

The beach at Previsa is something like one I once
visited in the Florida Keys—a long, hot strip of white
sand with thick vegetation springing up suddenly on
one side and the water sucking at the other, stretching
away in an aquamarine reverie. But the comparison
ends there, for the land of Greece is burdened with hills
and mountains that are ironic with age and agelessness,
old hags stooping and at the same time young brown
nubile bodies lying very still.

We stood on the edge of the shore with our feet in
the tepid water. Children were plopping out sand cas-
tles, fat women were panting under umbrellas, adoles-
cents were horsing around and necking when they could
—just as they did at our town beach in Connecticut five
thousand miles away. In fact, the lapping water and
beach shouts and transistor radios interlacing the Greek
romantic ballads with American rock 'n' roll music
made me nostalgic.

We advanced, looking down. Whereas at home the
water is frigid and green and opaque, this water was
therapeutically warm and transparent. We could see the
gray and green and purple weeds among spongy rocks
swaying as in a rock garden fantasy.

"Don't go over *there*," said Costas, pointing to our right, where there was a sign in Greek I could not understand nailed up on a tall stick. "There are huge holes there where the Nazis bombed ships and supply movements."

At our own beach, I thought, no holes except by nature: innocent treachery. I am hungry, bread and mustard, bodies curling in the horrible ecstasy of starvation in Omonoia Square. My body. My mother's— Come off it, too many novels.

We slid easily into the water, without the shock of the dash and flip necessary to enter the Atlantic. And then we were children. Cavorting. Spitting water in a fountain overhead into the stone blood yellow of the Mediterranean sun. Water dripped salt into my eyes and mouth: same salt, same water, same origin. I shouted to Costas in English, "You old son of a bitch, you, I love Greece and America and life!" Costas looked puzzled, made a fast little circle next to his temple with an index finger: one is universally crazy, no doubt. He spit a good gush of water into my eyes, and I tackled him. We were a tangle of muscle and hair and limbs, and we came up gasping and laughing, splashing. We walked toward shore until the water was only up to our knees. We were not talking, each in his own world. Costas grew serious and stood apart, dripping. He was looking at the sign above the bomb holes. I knew what he was thinking. And I thought, too, of the night a month before at Ioannina when he had told me about it.

Ioannina is perhaps sixty winding mountain-road miles north of Previsa, thirty miles inland, and is the capital of the state of Epirus, where my parents were born. It is a town at the same time beautiful and ugly, situated by a giant green lake, mountains, crude farms. You can see the Turkish influence in life and architecture: minarets and painted yellow stone houses with red tile roofs, poverty, donkeys with loads of twigs, people drinking ponies of ouzo and tiny cups of strong, sweet Turkish coffee under the pines at the open tavernas on the square. You walk up and down the square in the early evening, with all of the townsfolk lolling, taking their evening *voltes;* there is no television, little money, contentment, laziness, the mountains tenaciously cupping all of the town in a valley of ancient malaise and peace.

Such was a large portion of my heritage. And as Costas and I strolled up and down the square arm in arm (there is no awkward American shame, but a warm feeling of friendship and humanity), he said, "Why are you here? All right, as a tourist, but you stay so long, living with your cousin. You are content to stay here and live as we do and give up your American luxuries?"

"I give up those for these other, more natural luxuries. And I am here to see what I came from, my origin. I want to go back to what was the beginning of me before New England and Pilgrims and the Revolution and the Civil War and Monroe Doctrine and war bonds—no, I am not clear to you. I mean before my American history. What about the mystery, the icon in our dining room with the Virgin staring at me with huge dolorous eyes, telling me all the times I stared at her since I was a little boy that kick-the-can and Franklin Roosevelt and central heating and 'Oh Beautiful For Spacious Skies' are not entirely mine, nor I theirs. You frown. I don't blame you, with my awkward mixture of Greek and English. I want to see my other ethos, the other ethnic part of me. You do understand."

And so we walked and talked, originally intending to go to one of the outdoor-chair movies and watch a foreign film (Greeks generally loathe Greek movies for their dullness and contrivance) under the stars, with the cool night air moving through the poplars against the bordering fences. But we continued to talk and gesture, and the people thinned out.

Costas said, "I bet I have a past more tragic than yours."

"I bet you don't. Tell me about it."

We had come to that point where he was losing the reticence that is behind the beginning of many relationships in the Mediterranean. He was opening up because he knew that I was not making fun of him, or being an American Braggart slumming. We were gradually trusting each other.

He spoke straight and simply. "When I was eight years old, my father was killed by the Germans in our public square along with five others as an example for someone's sabotage. I saw him brought home dead, ripped and bleeding. He was a wonderful, strong man, handsome, powerful, omnipotent, and I was his sun, he often said. I have had dreams of him, so many times, helping me, holding me, rubbing my head as I fall asleep in his lap. And he goes away. I wake up reaching for him, reaching out, calling, Father, come back!—and they killed him. They said his last word was freedom. Ha.

"My mother suffered and sacrificed bringing up my sister and brother and me all through the war. I am actually from Arta, and there we had a farm and a big orange grove. Both were taken away from us, first by the Germans, then by the Greek government, and now we own only a small piece of each. But it was mine, all of it. It was my father's, and it is my birthright, goddamit."

"Where is your communal farm code?" I said. He laughed.

"Anyway, that is my life," he said, too coldly, "no

father, hunger, and dispossession. Can you beat that?"

I said, nearly blurted, "My parents came to New England before I was born. My father has worked hard seven days a week all his life. My mother has been dead since I was three years old, and my brothers and sisters, five of us, have always lived home."

"Oh," Costas said, not wanting me to continue, holding his hand up to stop me. His soft dark eyes looked deeply into mine and then at the cobblestones in a kind of embarrassment. "The mother. You win then, yes. You win."

For, in Greece a boy loves his mother very much without the necessity of proclaiming a Mother's Day. She is an integral part of his life always, even after he marries.

I wanted to go on. I wanted to flood the square with sad tidings of no joy, of the paradox and irony in the freedom of no discipline and no mother love forever, ineradicable, a constant. But I knew that Costas understood.

We walked, sat at a little iron table painted blue, and ate bits of fried pepper, *feta,* and olives and bread as hors d'oeuvres, and drank the exquisite bittersweet, anise-tasting ouzo. We got up dizzy and meandered up and down the *plateía* some more, talking, comparing our army and civilian experiences. I said, finally, "If you are an orange grower and still have your farm in Arta, then why are *you* in Ioannina?"

It was hard for him, but now we had a bond of mutual sorrow and self-pity, we believed in each other, and he said: "Two years ago, in Arta, a dumb girl who was not so dumb seduced me and then told her father that I had deflowered her against her will, and I was forced to marry her. I hated her. I still do hate her. Everyone in the village knew that she was an easy mark from way back, but none of my friends who had had her

55

could or would go against the word of her father, who is a petty government official. And I had no father to stand up for me.

"After we were married, she tormented me. She wanted me to love her, to accept her as my wife with a real place in our home. My mother put her out in the barn, and she slept with the goats. She still does. She tried continually to seduce me again, because if she became pregnant, it would be all over for me. But I wouldn't. I told her to keep away from me, and I threatened her. She continued to bother me, and one day I bought a gun. I don't think I really would have killed her, but I'm not sure.

"One blinding hot afternoon, she came to me and said I want you, and started to undress before me right there under the trees. She is a beautiful girl and has a body that makes me melt now with passion even as it fills me with utter hate. I don't know now whether it was the heat or desire or hate, but I took out the pistol and said I'm going to kill you. I fired twice above my head. She ran away screaming.

"The police arrested me, and I was sentenced to jail here in Ioannina for two years for shooting a weapon with intent to kill. I have been out for five months, working as a plasterer, living with my cousins, who are, you know, friends of your cousin."

He stopped and put his hands over his eyes. "I don't know," he said, "whether I wanted to kill her or not. I may be evil. That's what haunts me, whether or not I'm evil, and what I'm living for."

"No, you're good, or you would have done it," I said. But what could I tell him? He really wanted to hear no judgment. He had made up his mind about his afflictions.

I asked him why he didn't go back and divorce her. She wouldn't give him a divorce. He was staying here purposely. He had a couple of friends spying on her for him, and she would break down soon, she was that sexual, and he would have proof of adultery, go back, divorce her, and live his life on his bit of farm.

We finished the night sitting in the deserted new upper *plateia,* where a small fountain has been built that has colored lights flashing on the dancing spray of water at night: a rather discordant and absurd bit of modernity. Now we sat on the cold stone benches, I shivering, for I am considerably thinner than Costas. The water had long since stopped in the fountain. The petunias and zinnias were lurid under the weak lamppost lights, and the nocturnal dampness had fallen down from the mountains.

Looking at the new tiles on the square, I said, "You mean to tell me that a man who lays these squares should get as much money as a skilled surgeon?"

"To each his share as he labors," said Costas.

"Then a popular whore should make millions." We laughed.

The cold stars were falling thick in clusters around us. I said, "Why do we argue anyway, when all of it, the whole thing, is pointless?" And the stars fell, cracked like quartz, sprinkled all over the man-made, Marxist-capitalist tiles.

I stood staring down at the water, at the ferns and polyps, weeds and rocks, and I could still see fragmented stars on the tiles of the square at Ioannina. I felt again the cold of the night and shivered violently under the sun of the Previsa afternoon.

"Are you chilled?" Costas asked, flipping his hair back.

"No, not at all," I said. I was sweating.

"Do you feel very strong?"

"Why?"

"What do you say we swim out to that bell buoy?"
He pointed out into the bay.

It did not seem far away. My thoughts had left me
torpid. Costas was eager, full of energy.

"But I'm a little hungry," I said.

"Eat when we come in. Otherwise, you'll get
cramps. Besides, you *can* be hungry. You have your freedom." He poked me.

"*Touché.* O.K., then. *Páme.*"

"*Pamé,*" he said, laughing. These are the slang
initials of the Communist Party in Greece, and a kind
of slogan-pun, since *páme* means Let's go.

We swam strongly at first, then more leisurely. As
we got farther out, we kept changing our pace: crawl,
backstroke, sidestroke. The sun was benevolent in water
that was becoming cooler as we progressed.

Casual. Lolling swim. No pressure. Costas and I
alternated the lead, and we stopped now and then to
exchange a few comments. I told him the last one
to the bell buoy is a rotten egg, and explained that to
him, and he spoke of a donkey's tail.

Costas said, "Have you ever been afraid of drowning?"

"No, never."

"Nor have I."

"I grew up on the shore," I said. "The water is the
dominant force of my life. Even my zodiac says so."

"Do you believe that garbage?"

"No, but the stars. I look at them, at their distance, their mystery and beauty, and I believe in *them.*
I even long for them."

"You should become an astronaut, or a saint,
then."

At one point we tested the water for depth: neither of us could touch bottom no matter how hard we
tried. As I plunged downward, the water became a

block of impenetrable ice, and with bursting lungs, I pumped to the surface. I had swallowed water, and I gagged at its salinity. Relaxing, we continued to swim.

At last the bell buoy loomed up, huge, painted red and yellow metal, conical, ponderous, bobbing in a friendly way, not really a bell buoy at all, but something like a nun buoy with a light at the top of its cone. We kept moving toward it, intending to hang on to it for a while, rest, then head back into shore.

It would not be long now. It certainly would be a relief. I was tired, felt a stitch in my side develop and subside. It seemed hours since we had sat drinking beer and arguing. Was that this very day? Costas had guts. But if he was willing to swim out here, then so was I. And what was there to lose?

While thinking in rhythmic sections of sentences as I stroked, I struggled ahead. I kept looking at the buoy intensely. I swam, stopped, looked at it. Mechanically, I swam some more, watching it as it swelled, rolled, barely moved, rolled again, glistened, and then dulled. I knew its thick bottom, slender rise, all of its cutout squares, niches, graceful narrowing at the top like a wimple. And in this constant staring, my neck was stiffening from being in a continuous arch, from looking at the buoy, from not being able to take my eyes off it.

Something insidious began, illusory, slow, and almost with a frightening majesty. Rhythmically, pointing like a magnet to the core of my soul, the buoy was drawing me, luring me, possessing me. All other elements ebbed. Reaching the buoy seemed the only goal of my life. Incredibly, the buoy became the only reason I was alive. It seemed, in a hypnotic way, perfectly logical, rational. I forgot my family, home, my friends, my trip, or where I was. I forgot even how not long before, playing with Costas near the shore, I had thought myself madly in love with life. And as I stared at the buoy, I was thinking how it would be when I reached it, what it would feel like: rough and hard and chipped, and it might even scrape my skin, bruise me. As I embraced it, I would not mind the hurt. I would be so grateful for having got to it.

To get to it faster with the most power, I swam the crawl until my arms ached, always trying to keep the buoy directly before me, and ending up forty or fifty feet to the west of it, drifting strongly toward the bay's mouth far away. In this frustration, my logic returned and said to me, You will never reach that buoy.

"The current," said Costas. "It's too strong."

"We can make it," I said, slightly delirious. "It's not too far now."

It was then that I looked back to land for the first time with any real comprehension. What I saw alarmed me: the shore was at least two miles away. The people on the beach were a mass of tiny colored dots, the trees a thick and menacing jungle closing out the world of land, fencing in the whole shore and sea. My sympathetic nervous system tried to set up a condition of panic in me, panic about the distance and being out of earshot, about drowning and cramps and sharks and death. But by waiting in a kind of desperation for it to pass, I did not let the panic eat me alive. I treaded water, then shouted to Costas, who was even farther out toward the hungry mouth of the bay, "We can still do it, I think."

Costas shook his head, with a serious look clouding his face. I struggled with all I had, flailing, kicking, feeling the heat in my face, and in my mind I was swearing, Goddamit, I will do it.

The water, once so romantic and caressing and warm, was a monster, a cold harpy with amorphous hands. I kept my eyes fixed on the buoy as on a miracle about to occur—the friendly buoy nodding and bowing to me, a priest saying, Why, yes, my son, come right into the basilica. Suddenly it became a hideous priest smirking at me, an evil old priest with gaps in his teeth where the open metal ribbing was, and he took me into the church. And then, where two large bolts had been on the face of the buoy, right there were the tragic eyes of the Virgin in the icon, yes, that was she, I *saw* her—the gold Virgin with her red veil, bowing her head regally, tears in her heart, withholding always a mystery from me, keeping love inside her, unable to give me that love and the answer to her mystery. I was hypnotized, treading water, wondering at the death of her, of her coaxing me toward her, knowing always that I ought never to reach her. She must never take me. Yet I was trying desperately to get to her.

"No," I shouted in English, "I don't want you!"

"What is it?" said Costas. "What's wrong with you?"

"It is the *Panaghía*," I said in Greek.

"No," he said, laughing. "It looks like a stupid cop." Then he looked bemused. "But no, no. Wait. I know." His face brightened. "Look. It's God Himself!"

Neither of us believed in God, and the relief of his comment at once had us laughing hysterically in the water two or three miles from land, not far from the brown reclining mountains—two lost children floundering and not lost, united in aloneness, love, and the unspoken possibility of death.

Gushing up out of the water, we were two tan strong boys laughing at God the Buoy, at themselves, the water, the universe, I pointing my finger and saying in English, "Go on home, ya dirty old man, g'wan home—"

Sometimes the buoy tried to become again for me the Virgin and for him the policeman. But Costas was right—first through humor and then through delirium and horror, it *was* God, it was the Unknown and Uncaring God in His Unknown and Uncaring holy water, with the priestesses lying around brown and splendid, and far away His ant people crawling and sunning on the white strip.

We were drifting out fast. "Come on," Costas said, "let's go. He doesn't want me, that bastard, and I don't want Him either. I tried, but He doesn't care. Let's go."

We began sidestroking, backstroking, dogpaddling back. The shore was perhaps two hundred and fifty thousand miles away. We swam for at least five hundred hours.

"We won't make it," I said to Costas. He did not answer.

We will, we won't, I thought, what difference does it make. "Goodbye, God," I shouted.

After more swimming that was becoming more and more pointless, Costas said, "I feel a cramp starting in my leg." His teeth were clenched, his blue lips pulled, stretched apart.

"I'll help you," I said. But I couldn't have done a thing.

"No, it will go away."

We swam as relaxed as we could, flopping our water-wrinkled hands before us methodically.

We are not going to make it, I thought. I won't shout for help. Perhaps someone on the shore has seen us and sent a boat out to save us. Perhaps not. So what.

I did not fully believe in my indifference, and I felt somehow guilty about it. Nevertheless, it was within this guilt that I felt peacefully isolated: the people on shore were such a long way off that my mind shut them out. They're so far away, I thought, my words moving osmotically between me and the water as though we were one organic thing. They're so far away that they won't help me if I shout. They can't help. And even if they can, I don't care. I don't want to shout for help. I don't have the urge to shout for help, to shout, to help.

Then there was nothing: no Costas, not even a bird, nor the possibility of a boat, nor a mountain, nor ocean, nor sun—only a peaceful state of limbo, a feeling of floating on my back, floating nowhere within nothing.

There was no time nor noise nor reality until the sun came back to me. It had moved down through the tremulous sky what seemed a half foot, and then I knew that something called time had passed and acted on me.

I heard the water slopping around me. I looked: Costas was fifteen feet away, floating on his back. He glanced at me, and his face was like a statue's—passionless, with blue lips, full of the sun.

Brave Costas, I thought. He hasn't panicked, even in pain.

We drifted rapidly. I felt the current getting stronger, pulling us greedily. The sun was a long yellow stick clubbing at our heads. The land lay five or six miles away, hazy, a mirage.

Go ahead and panic, I said to myself, see if I care.

"Are you all right, Costas?" I asked.

"Yes."

He was wincing. His leg must have been killing him.

And then, rather foolishly, I asked, "Do you care?"

He looked at me for a long time, and then said, "Of course I care, or I wouldn't be doing it." It was like the punch line of a shaggy-dog story. "But why are you so grim, so dramatic?" He broke into a childish, sly smirk.

"Because I don't believe in this," I said. "But I don't believe in the other, either."

"Believe and believe," said Costas. "Have fun. Make a joyful noise unto the Lord!" And with that he let out a cry that had more agony, more loneliness and pain and anguish in it than any other human noise I have ever heard, before or since. It made me animal-frightened, it made me want to weep, it made me crave and detest humanity.

Then there was a long silence, broken by Costas' chuckling and saying, "Listen. I hear them—the seraphim and the devils coming for us."

The noise was a hum, a beating of wings, and I believed him. It became a fierce buzz, then a bursting whine.

I squinted and shielded my eyes: a small red and gold caïque with sails drawn and with a big outboard motor seemed right on top of us. I did not shout for joy. Perhaps I had always known that this boat was going to come. Perhaps not. I really didn't give a damn, or so it seemed then, once the boat was already there.

"We are saved," Costas said, with absolutely no emotion in his voice, his eyes, his face.

The boat suddenly slowed down its motor.

"Please, into shore will you take us?" I shouted in broken Greek syntax.

The boat was beside us. There were two men, and the one in the stern cut the motor. Neither offered a hand. I climbed up, then struggled to get Costas aboard. He could hardly move his right leg.

The boat contained a big net of dripping, glistening fishes. The stink of life, of the life of the sea, made me shudder.

The skinny man on the outboard said, "What the hell were you doing way out here?" I turned to Costas, who shrugged his shoulders.

"We were looking for girls," I said in English.

The man frowned. "Foreigner?" he said to Costas, who nodded.

The man raised his eyebrows, gawked for a second, then revved up the engine. The boat moved slowly under its cargo. In about ten minutes we were gliding by our tall buoy twenty feet away.

Neither of us spoke. Shivering, we watched it as we passed.

I tried to see it genuflecting, bowing, sloughing off its outer robes of blue water, sighing. But no, the *Panaghia* was gone, and I was glad of it. The buoy was now merely that—a buoy, painted red and yellow, indifferent, marking the current, moving rhythmically with the water's indifferent movement.

We churned through thicker and thicker weeds. The man standing before me in the bow, tall and muscular and tanned oily black, with a fat drooping mustache, wearing a sticky cap and torn trousers, in bare feet, looked first at Costas, then at me, and muttered, "Foolish, stupid brats." He spat on the deck and said no more. He was heroic in stature, beautiful, serene.

Exhausted, trailing a hand in the fast-warming water, I looked at Costas. His face was blazing. His head was a mass of shining clusters of wet curls. His eyes were immense and black and on fire. He was smiling at me with the thin, sad smile of the saints in Byzantine icons.

I turned to the shore and watched the people come up out of a variegated blur as though someone had focused them under a huge microscope.

The Pigeon

CLARA SAT IN A chrome-and-plastic chair on her porch in a small New England town. All the lights were out in the house. She liked it that way. With her five children married and gone, she felt at peace in the dark. Moths were flying around the street light, and fireflies were pulsating in the dark lot of wild growth and trees next to the house. Nothing looked clear. She was dreaming and listening to the crickets.

A car came racing down the hill, its headlights up bright, lighting the tops of maple trees. It crackled on the sandy macadam road as it slowed in front of the house. Clara stood up in the darkness of the porch, ready to fly into the house. She was barefoot. She pushed a rough braid of dull gray hair over her shoulder, and tried to smooth her unironed dress. She fingered a string of white beads that dangled over the front of her old cardigan. Squinting, she recognized the car; it belonged to Paolo, her youngest son. The front door opened on the passenger side. A heavy-set man got out. It was him—her husband, Dominic. He spoke a few words and shut the door. The car pulled away skidding.

Perhaps if she were very still, he would not notice her. He had threatened yesterday, when she had taken the pigeon upstairs, and again this morning, to take the bird away from her. She had been foolish to tell him about it. Maybe he would think she was asleep and go straight past the porch to the back door and in to bed. But no. Ah, the nuisance. He stopped at the other side of the porch rail. He was still quite strong, his hair was white, his face almost black with suntan from working in his vegetable garden out back. She stood flat against the wall of the house, hanging on to her beads.

"Still up?" he asked in Italian. They always spoke in their native language. His voice, as always, was loud. "It's after eleven."

Her heart was beating fast. She could hardly see him; he looked like a white shirt and a pile of white silk hair floating by themselves in the dark.

He got right to the point. He said, "Paolo says you can't keep it. He says it's not healthy. He says we got to let it go or else stick it in a cage in back of the garage, but then we'll have plenty of troubles with the zoning laws and the cops when the neighbors find out. He says it's best if we get rid of it anyway—it will make you sick." Dominic laughed, and Clara could see his big teeth. He said, "Paolo says you are quite a character, catching a pigeon."

Clara spoke rapidly. "It was no trouble. I was hanging a towel on the line and the pigeon flew down from the sky and walked up to me, and I bent over and picked him up. He liked me. I wanted him, I took him to my room. So what of that?"

Dominic said, "Well, we got to let it go—right now. It'll only get you sick up in that closed, hot room." He went along the side of the house, and in through the back door. She heard him bump against the table in the kitchen—the clumsy old fool—and she heard the light switch go on at the foot of the stairs. Then he was climbing them slowly, as if he didn't want to go up, or was tired.

She stood on the porch for a moment and thought, Why didn't my baby—my Paolo—come in, or wave, or say hello? Then she went into the house through the front screen door. It slammed behind her. She padded through the dark living room and kitchen and went upstairs. Her bedroom was at the top of the landing, directly above her husband's room. The door was open, and the light was on. It was more powerful than the hall light, and it made a hard glare. She could hear a scraping and clucking sound coming from the room.

Clara stood in the doorway. The veins in her right leg hurt, and she held the heel of that foot up off the floor a little. Dominic was crouched down, his face almost touching the floor. Ah, the buffoon. Clara wanted to laugh, but he would have heard her. Moving his short, heavy arms, he was scraping a broom under the bed. He clucked with his tongue and made a sucking noise with his lips. She thought, What does he think he is calling—a dog? "Some of his smaller feathers are falling out," she said.

There was a whirring and a scrambling noise under the bed, and Dominic slid the broom swiftly across the floor.

"Some of his smaller *feathers* are falling out."

"Yes, I heard you. It's sick." He held up one tough palm, looked up at her, frowning, and said, "It was standing away far over in the corner, all puffed up. And it hasn't even touched this bread you have here." He turned his mouth down and said, *"Mamma mia."* He added some light curse words. His black eyes flashed. He looked under the bed, grunting, and again he scraped the broom in an arc. "Stupid. Foolish thing," he said, and pulled himself up on his knees. He pushed on his

68

back with one hand and said, "Oh." The blood was heavy in his face, and the wrinkles in his forehead were deep and sweaty.

Clara stood in silence. She shut her eyes and the moment shifted. She was twelve years old. She thought, When Mama goes down to the well for water, then I'll sneak it some corn.

Dominic turned the broom around, got down, pushed it once more, and swept the bird out. "There!" he said. Flapping by, the bird stepped into a cup of water that had been set down by one of the legs of the headboard. Dominic let the broom fall to the floor with a loud smack, and he swung forward. "Got you," he said, wrapping his big hands around the bird. It struggled. He held it tight and grinned. It tried to flap, and shuddered, moving its head in jerking motions. Then it was still for a minute.

Clara bent her head in pity, staring at the pigeon. It was gray, with one of its big red claws sticking out from under Dominic's hands. Around the throat, it was shining blue and cerise and silver, and it had a deep-blue head. Its eye was a tiny copper disk within a clear globe, with a black, wild-staring spot in the center. Clara put her hands together over her face.

"It's beautiful, all right," Dominic said. He groaned as he got to his feet.

Clara uncovered her face. She saw the veins beating at her husband's temple.

The pigeon struggled once more, with its claw splayed, and almost got away. Dominic moved out into the hall. Talking softly to the bird, he clomped down the stairs in his thick shoes and baggy black pants. Clara followed. He went out the front door, holding the bird high before him. The door banged. Clara went through, and it banged again. Dominic went down the porch steps, and Clara walked close in procession behind him, her arms stretched out, her hands together, mocking him. She moved with a slight lurch, her white beads swinging heavily, her braid flopping at her back. How I hate you, you vile one, she thought. Immediately, feeling guilty and afraid, she put her hand to her mouth. Then she smirked.

Dominic lumbered through the lot next to the house; his shoes swished in the dry grass.

Surrounded by the noise of crickets that ceased and started hesitantly, Clara walked behind her husband among the trees to the far end of the lot. Branches and twigs bent and snapped. Fireflies sparked in clusters. Remembering that other bird, Clara thought, I must let it go before Mama kills it for supper. She smelled strong, wild honeysuckle, and it nearly made her faint.

Under shadowy leaves, Dominic stopped and released the pigeon. It flopped to the ground. Dominic bent down, cursing, and felt in the weeds until he found it. This time, he threw the bird up in the air. "Go!" he commanded, and it flapped and floated down, disappearing among the thickets.

Clara wanted to cry. The pigeon. Her secret pet, cooing under a crude cupboard in the family hovel of her childhood village near Naples.

"That's all," Dominic said, brushing his hands together. "Birds carry diseases. It would have made you sick." He put his arm around his wife's shoulders, and they stood hidden together for a moment. Even in old age she was taller than he, and that fact flashed into her mind now. She was conscious of the appearance they must always have made together. She laughed gutturally. He said, "That's the way," and patted her back. They walked through the heavy grass in silence, back to the house.

70

With her head lowered, Clara followed Dominic upstairs again. He got the broom and, breathing heavily,
swept up, making a pile of dry, hard, white bread and
feathers. "Get the dustpan," he said.

She went down, got it, and came back. Climbing
the stairs slowly, she thought, Cruel, cruel. She twisted
the pigeon's neck behind the village hut. "They won't
get you now," she said. She stroked the dead bird and
wept. Quickly, under the hot sun, she dug a hole in the
stony earth and buried the bird behind the outhouse.
No one will ever know, she thought as she reached the
top of the stairs, cradling the red metal dustpan in her
arms. She went into her room and handed it to Dominic
without looking at him.

He swept up the debris. "Look," he said, "the
poor thing never ate a crumb. It would have perished."

"He will perish in the darkness," Clara said,
closing her wet eyes, shaking her head. She felt exhausted.

"No. It's got a better chance outside."

"A better chance," Clara said.

Her husband took the cup of water into the bathroom across the hall and emptied it. "You must wash
this cup in boiling water," he said.

"In boiling water," she repeated.

He went to her room, picked up the full dustpan
and the broom, and started slowly down the stairs. She
began to follow.

"No," he said, looking up. His face was black and
scowling in the dim light of the stairwell. Big drops of
sweat shone on his forehead. "You go to bed now. It's
late. And don't bring no more goddam animals in the
house." Then after a pause he said softly, "You understand, eh?"

She whimpered.

He continued down the stairs. "I'm going to bed

myself," he said to the bottom step. "Don't worry. It'll be all right out there." He turned his face up to her and said good night.

"Why didn't Paolo come in to see me?" Clara cried out.

"He had to go pick up his wife from the bingo. Why do you bother me?"

She put her hand over her mouth, repressing another whimper, trying to have some dignity.

"Go to bed now," Dominic said. "Tomorrow night, Paolo will come. Or Mary or Tommy or somebody, and they will take you for a ride and get you some ice cream."

Tomorrow night, she thought, and shook her head. She went to her room and undressed. She put on a pink, flowered nightgown and undid the braid of hair. She heard Dominic knocking the dustpan against the trash can in the back hall. She waited, her thin lips hanging open. The light switch snapped off in the kitchen. He shuffled through and shut off the light at the bottom of the stairs. The hall went black. A relief. Below, Dominic muttered, "It would have croaked in there."

She heard a click as he turned the ceiling light on in his room. She sat on her bed and combed out her hair with a big comb. She felt lighter. He would lie there now on the double bed that had been theirs, and read the Italian paper and smoke one of his crooked little black cigars. Then he would cough for a while. Before going to sleep, he might go to the kitchen for some wine. Maybe his light would still be on in the morning —maybe not. These days, nothing was sure. What ever had been? That he had loved her with the light on and with the light off, with and without cigar and wine breath. When? Oh, when had that been? Trembling, she put out the light, crossed herself, and lay down on the bed. At once, her legs began to ache and throb.

After a long time, she could see in the room. Shadows of leaves moved on one wall. The crickets sang outside. Downstairs, Dominic began coughing.

Clara smiled, dreaming herself toward sleep. Someday, she would get away from this dirty hovel. She would marry. She would love her husband, and he would love her. And no one would ever find out. After all, they would have killed and eaten him. Or he would have perished, that beautiful bird, in darkness.

Love and Wisdom

M Y MOTHER DIED of a renal disease when I was
eleven, leaving my father and six sons. When
I was nine, the local welfare agency had placed
the three youngest in a foster home in Rock Point, a village just west of here on the Connecticut shoreline. The
agency had acted on neighbors' reports of negligence. I
was third-oldest, and glad that I did not have to go. My
mother had become ill when I was six. Since then, I had
been virtually my own boss. I thrived on my small-city
life of freedom among the tenements, alleys, and back
lots, in movie houses, on the sidewalks, the docks, the
beaches. I enjoyed reading whatever I could get my
hands on and as late as I chose in the back bedroom of
our long, dirty apartment. I wrestled with my next-older
brother, moved through the warmth, order, and security
of school as though life had meaning and coherence,
and played games—from king-of-the-mountain to near-
endless bouts of Monopoly on rainy days—with my
neighborhood friends, who were Syrian, Italian, and
Irish. We were Greek.

The week after my mother died, my two older
brothers, afraid and bereaved, and I, who felt only confused, were sent to a suburb of Boston for a week, to
live with a distant cousin from Greece while my father

settled his affairs. All I remember about that trip is that I couldn't wait to get home again.

My father—tired, thin, paler even than he usually was—met us at the train and took us home. The change he had wrought in the apartment was unbelievable. The walls were painted in light colors, fresh curtains hung at the tall windows, bright flowered linoleum and pieces of new furniture decorated every room, and everything was clean. It was as though my mother's sickness had been synonymous with disorder, and now that she had died squalor had miraculously disappeared.

I went through the house like a bird in a sudden Eden. My two older brothers followed, and I couldn't understand their silence, their brooding. I didn't know, and I didn't find out until I was grown and respectful of the memory of my mother, what an attractive, good person she had once been; my brothers were remembering shadows of her when she had not been haggard and unkempt and miserably bitter.

My father told us to remain in the apartment for a while—he would be back shortly. We groaned, anxious to go out and play. At noon, he returned with a woman and told us that she would be taking care of us. Then he went back to work in his diner, which he still runs, twenty years later, even though there is hardly enough business to bother. Always a solemn man, he never spoke of my mother, never expressed—in our presence, at least—guilt, loneliness, or grief.

Like other men who had come from Greece to America, he used his wife harshly without knowing it was wrong. Here in a strange America, in the Depression, my mother had no family to turn to for solace or courage. And possibly my father came to neglect the two qualities that had (according to stories I've heard since from relatives) enchanted him—her shyness and her stark, untampered-with Mediterranean beauty—so that

75

she gradually lost them both. Once she was totally destroyed, my father closed up his life, opened his diner, and went faithfully to work ten hours a day, seven days a week, providing for his children, and did absolutely nothing else.

The woman he left that noon to care for us introduced herself as Ellen Slocum. She asked us our names. We told her in order: Thomas, Michael, and Terry Vallas. She said that she was sorry about our mother, that she well understood, having cared for her own poor mother when everyone else in the family had deserted her, until the end. Ellen told us that she would be cooking our meals and taking care of our beds and clothes. I think I was spellbound by even that much concern. She wanted to know if we had had our lunch. When we said no, she clucked her gums together and worked her mouth so that a fat little mole danced up and down on her dark cheek. She said something about not having asked our father if there was anything in the icebox. My oldest brother said listlessly that there were some eggs and Greek cheese. I can still remember his face that day; it was melancholy, lost—a dark, strong replica of our mother's face.

Ellen asked what Greek cheese was like. She hadn't any "notion" about Greek food, she said. She was a Yankee—her no-good father had been an Indian, and her mother Scotch-Irish American. Thomas got the little wooden vat of cheese out of the refrigerator and pried open the top with a table knife. Ellen, wrinkling her leathery face so that her gums showed and her dull black eyes disappeared under the flesh of her high cheeks, said that it stank and she wasn't going to cook that stuff. We didn't say anything. She put her hand on my head gently and rumpled my hair a little, almost caressed it, and asked if I didn't think the cheese stank, too. I looked at my brothers, and they looked back at me. I didn't answer. Thomas, who was fifteen, volunteered to cook. He said that for his part he *loved* Greek cheese. Michael instantly agreed. Ellen told us to wash our hands if we were to eat.

We went through the long dark hall back to the bathroom, smirking and giggling as we went. Wash our hands to eat? What for? What were we—sissies? In the bathroom, Thomas quietly announced that he didn't like her. Michael didn't either. I said that she was chubby, and we went back to the kitchen. Thomas got the food ready, scrambling the cheese and eggs together in olive oil. I had always loved this food. When Ellen put it on the plates, she let us know once more that it certainly stank. She smoothed the back of my hair as I ate, and smiled at me. She said, "Don't it stink, Terry?" I looked at her, then at my two brothers across from me, and, somewhat ruefully, said yes.

Life fell into an incredibly organized pattern of school, normal meals, and sleep. I hardly ever saw my father. My brothers soon became alienated from me and from the house. Ellen gave orders, shouted curfews (which my brothers chafed at bitterly), and took excellent care of us. After a couple of months, at the request of the welfare agency and in response to my own pleadings, she moved from her uptown furnished room and came to live with us.

I devoured her love like a savage. My brothers were strategic enemies, my father was a stranger. Until then, I had been a cunning man-child who had learned at first hand the indifference of the world, and somehow I knew even then that Ellen had not. She was a naïve fifty-six-year-old spinster, with rough working hands, and black wiry hair mixed with gray, which she wore pulled back in a thick bun. Whatever she said, I vocally agreed with her. She said that men were no good, and I agreed. They were out for one thing only. I agreed. My father was stupid to have made that poor woman have all those children. I agreed.

Ellen took me places—on excursions to the five-and-ten, to an Irish maid friend's apartment for tea, to the movies, to a lonely cemetery three miles away, where she trimmed her mother's grave. For these outings, she wore a cloth turban and black thick-heeled, perforated shoes, and she carried a cloth bag. Holding her hand as we plodded down the hot streets, I exulted without knowing why—until a friend approached, when I undid my hand from Ellen's as unobtrusively as I could and felt embarrassed at my clean, mended clothes and new straw cap with its stupid little visor. My friend, as bedraggled as he had ever been, and I grumbled hello at each other and passed. Once he had disappeared, I took Ellen's hand again, smoldering in a sense of betrayal, of lost liberty and fun, of a shuddery thankfulness for Ellen. The last feeling usurped the others, wrenched me from a random field, and stabilized my life.

Ellen took me a few times to visit her younger sister, Mabel. She and her husband lived on a farm eight miles east of here. A town boy, I soaked up everything: lumbering dumb cows with their saliva hanging in silver threads, black-and-white stodgy bony calves, goats with horns that were hot and rough to the touch, flocks of noisy grubbing chickens, waddling dirty white ducks, potent dungheaps, scooped salt licks, and the yellowish intense stony hills that were used for pasture. I drank ice-cold goat's milk, helped Mabel's husband make butter, and examined with private joy the colors and smells in the vegetable and flower gardens. On the way home on the bus after one of these visits, I put my head against Ellen's arm. Looking out at the black sky full of stars, I told her my secret—that I was going to be a doctor some day. She seemed happy and encouraged me; she said that it would mean a lot of hard work. In the dark bus, getting sleepy, I said that it was so much fun to go places with her. Wearily, she said it was more fun to get home.

Home had become a warm and real place, and I spent most of my time there. Ellen washed and ironed and told me about working in a thread mill all of her younger years, to take care of her mother. She sang songs like "Wait Till the Sun Shines, Nellie" and "School Days" as she made strawberry shortcake, or cooked hot dogs, waffles, and Canadian bacon, or poached eggs for our tea. She spent some of the money my father paid her on this food and on our excursions, and she gave me pocket money out of her own pay, too. Evenings, while she sewed or embroidered, the sound of her vaulted wooden radio filled the living room with "Dr. Christian," "It Pays to Be Ignorant," "Suspense," "Lux Radio Theatre," and "The Lights Along the Shore." The last was a local Methodist-church program of hymns, announcements, get-well wishes, and sermonettes by the Reverend Francis Parkman Lake, who spoke in a voice I can still hear—resonant, strong, deep. It made me feel that there could never possibly be anything wrong again.

There *was* nothing wrong for a while. Perhaps Ellen occasionally punished me, and taught me manners that seemed useless and tedious. But she also bought me whimsical games and coloring books, watercolor sets, a pair of roller skates, which I had for two years desperately wanted and now ignored, and wonderful books to read—"Black Beauty," "Robinson Crusoe," "Hans Brinker." And she took care of me when I was sick, and made me laugh whenever life was bleak.

I was content in all of this lavish life, never letting on to her that even though on the surface I had become

79

a spoiled sissy, I was still a tough conniver, with as many old-time rotten words in my mind as ever, with a desire still to be part of the neighborhood gang and, like all the boys I knew, to swipe trinkets, destroy property, raid the few pear trees and grapevines we knew about, and indulge with them in sexual reveries far beyond our years. But the sacrifice of these pleasures was easy when they were weighed against warmth and care.

After a year, all harmony ceased. I should have been prepared. The chaos of the past should have kept me on guard. In May, just as I turned twelve, my father announced that he was going to take in a Greek woman to care for us. And it happened at a time when Ellen was disgusted with my brothers.

Michael had been breaking the curfew and secretly smoking; she had found half a pack of cigarettes in his dungarees in the laundry. But Thomas was the real thorn. In a rage, he had forced her out of his room one Saturday morning when she told him to get up because she wanted to wash the sheets. "You just want to lie in there thinking dirty things!" she accused him. Thomas didn't get angry easily, but I can see him that day, tall in his underwear, his face troubled with sleep and adolescent hurt. He shouted at her to get out of his room and stay out, her and her dirty mind. He slammed the door. I could hear him whimpering, and I grieved for him as Ellen trembled on her way down the hall, scolding about a "dirty picture" she had discovered in his bureau. She took my hand and pulled me along, and I felt anguish. I wanted to say that he was right, that she shouldn't have said that stuff to my brother, but I kept quiet, and loyalty and treason raised hell together inside of me. She hollered that she was leaving—she couldn't stand this insolent brat any longer who thought he was so "goddam handsome," or the other one, either, who was so "ornery" and disobedient.

At that, I put my arms around her warty, puffy neck and begged her not to go, ever, and never to leave me alone. I squeezed her corseted frame, I kissed her and cried, and she calmed me and gave me her word.

My father's decision moved swiftly through the house. In two weeks, Ellen was gone with all of her things. She had taken a position as housekeeper to an old couple in Rock Point. The world was disorder again. I realized that I was not the conniver I had assumed. Through kindness and order and discipline, I had actually learned to love someone. I brooded, desolate, in the back bedroom.

Summer came, and with it the old Greek woman. She was very kind, the godmother of my youngest brother. I tried to respond to her kindness, but it was no use. My father said that he wanted our home to be a *Greek* home, that we were to go regularly to St. Basil's Greek Orthodox church and have Greek food and talk Greek in our house. One Sunday, we had *moussaka* for dinner. I left it, whining for waffles or hot dogs or strawberry shortcake. I said that Greek cheese stank. My father slapped me. My brothers made disgusted faces and shook their heads. I thought they all hated me. The Greek woman tried to console me, but I ran out, took a bus to Rock Point, and visited Ellen in the funny house where she was staying. Among other things, the living room contained a grandfather's clock, a horsehair couch, tiffany-glass lamps, a Morris chair, and a small, light-walnut foot-pump organ. I ate Ellen's homemade applesauce and ginger cookies, and listened politely to the feeble couple she was taking care of. They went off to lie down, and Ellen and I went uptsairs to her room to talk. There was a drowsy, ticking silence. Sitting in a rocker on a braided rug, I told Ellen about my life without her. She said that she was unhappy, too. We wept, we embraced for a moment, trying to press the loneliness of life out of us in the silent, sun-filled room.

After, I walked in the heat down the highway half a mile to visit my brothers in the foster home. They were growing fast. The family melancholy seemed stamped into them beneath the veneer of play and fun. They began to understand that I was their brother. The foster mother, a widow whom they called Miss Ruth, seemed pleasant enough; I didn't know yet that she ruled by fear. Going home on the bus, I got the idea that I should live there. It would mean a restricted life again, but I would be near Ellen.

The next week, I went to the welfare office, found the social worker I remembered from the year before, and sat down to complain. I told her that the Greek woman was leaving (she was sick and did leave shortly after) and that there would be no one to take care of us. The social worker said that they had no intention of leaving me home anyway; I was vulnerable—whatever that meant.

My father got hold of me next evening and, pulling at my ear, asked why I had been complaining. My brothers called me a squealer. I said I didn't want to live in this lousy house anymore. My father shook me hard, his bony face and angry gray eyes close to me. He said to grow up, that I was a spoiled baby, and now look what I'd gone and done: the welfare office was going to place me a hundred miles away in a technical school for boys, to learn a trade.

A technical school for boys! A trade! I was going to be a *doctor*. I had made that decision at the age of nine while watching the family doctor attend my mother, and it had stuck. Nothing was going to interfere, either with that desire or with my desire to be near

Ellen. I went to the drugstore, telephoned Miss Ruth, and asked if I might be permitted to live there. A few more nights of swollen sorrows, a couple of visits more to the foster home and to the welfare office, and it was arranged. The night before I left home, my father and my big brothers got me in the kitchen. They said that I was consigning myself to a prison. They begged me to stay home, promising an allowance, all the books I wanted, the free life. And they pleaded with me to tell the meddlesome welfare office that I had been foolish, that I was all right and could live perfectly well at home. I wouldn't listen. I thought it was a plot—that they knew I wanted to be near Ellen and were out to ruin my plan.

I moved into the foster home with cardboard boxes full of clothes, books, and playthings. I felt lost and guilty, but somehow incredibly hopeful. After all, Ellen was half a mile away, and I wasn't at some technical school a hundred miles from home.

I visited Ellen often during August. In September, when school opened, Miss Ruth said that I could see Ellen just on weekends, and only in the foster home. Ellen came and sat sulking, visiting in a kitchen full of children. She stayed long, and at the end of her visit kissed me. I drew back a little, confused, while Miss Ruth sat watching with a deadly expression on her face. For there was no love in the foster home.

The next day, Miss Ruth asked me if I had ever slept in the same bed with Ellen. I quite innocently said that I had. If I had a cold, she rubbed my chest with Vicks ointment, put a piece of flannel over that, and kept me near her to give me medicine. And a couple of times I'd had violent nightmares and got into her bed for the rest of the night. As soon as I told Miss Ruth, I knew I had admitted to the wrong thing. My innocent sleep, along with the great constant concern and praise I had for Ellen, and the presents from her I showed my little brothers (and gave them as I grew detached and older), convinced Miss Ruth that Ellen was unhealthy for me. Finally, she concluded that Ellen had a motive, and she barred her from visiting altogether. Ellen was using me, Miss Ruth said, waiting for the day when I would be old enough to support her in her old age. I thought that was preposterous, but I didn't dare say so. The technical school loomed.

Ellen tried to call me on the telephone. Miss Ruth, maneuvering to establish discipline, intercepted all calls and forbade her to talk to me. The foster mother, so abstract in my mind now, a white-haired, faceless woman in a cotton housedress, sat there in her mahogany dining room holding the phone, with the morning light coming through lace curtains illuminating her as if she were a huge Flemish scullery maid in an oil painting. She said into the phone, with a Yankee twang, that Ellen absolutely could never see me again and that was final. Then, triumphantly, she told me that if I ever conspired to see Ellen and she found out about it, she'd immediately have me sent to the technical school. Later that day, Miss Ruth said, "You don't feel bad about not being able to see her, now, do you?" I said no. She said that I knew Ellen was not good for me, didn't I? I said yes.

That night, unable to sleep, I sat in the dark at the dormer window of my room upstairs and stared at the stars bunched up over the road where I knew Ellen lived with no one who cared about her. Another betrayal. And this time because of that goddam school. It had become a threat to my life, a permanent Damocles' sword, and I fell under the spell of it even to the point of a final betrayal.

One afternoon late in September, I was walking home from school down a narrow country road. I was with a few other seventh-graders. A crowd of shouting small children was behind me, my younger brothers among them. I thought I heard my name called faintly. I turned but saw no one. I heard the voice again. It came from the bushes, a tall grove of lilac on the side of the hot tar road. "Terry," it said. "Here." I saw Ellen crouched in the mass of twigs and leaves. She beckoned. Was it a sad dream? The blood was drained from her face. She looked like a scared, turbaned witch crooking her finger at me. In a paroxysm, I loved her and I feared her. I wanted to talk to her, to tell her so many lonely things, but my brothers, the other children— someone would tell. That school! I kept going. I ran out ahead of the crowd, down a long hill, green tin lunch-box banging hollow against my leg. The leaves were beginning to turn, the sky was stark blue, the cicadas and crickets were screaming in the dry brush. I can still smell the hot wild grapes on their yellowing vines that clung to the trees along the road. Sweating, I reached the main highway. My side hurt. I ran past sculptured blasted-granite ledges, motionless oak trees, road banks. I kept saying in my mind, "I'm sorry, I couldn't help it, I had to. . . . I'm sorry, I couldn't help it, I had to."

I turned into our little road, went inside the house. I called Miss Ruth. She was down in the cellar, canning tomatoes. I took the stairs three at a time. Struggling for breath, I told her what had happened. "You did the right thing," she said, her hair a massive spun-glass halo as she sat in a black chair, holding a big wooden ladle. I knew I had not done the right thing, and I shivered in the dark cellar.

Fifteen minutes later, after my brothers had come clattering in and been told to be quiet, we watched through a tiny dirty window as Ellen marched by between two groups of schoolchildren on the highway. Her head was erect and thrust a little forward. The cinder-block wall before me looked thick and constraining. Yet a small part of whatever soul I had left went through to Ellen as she disappeared behind the elderberry bushes on the corner.

Two days later, I received an unsigned letter from her. I can still see the words in her strange cuneiform hand:

> *You are a skunk Terry and so is the woman who is staying with you. You forget all I did for you when you had no one.*

With the letter was a black-and-gray school photograph of me at eleven, torn into small squares.

After almost six years of a totally suppressed life, I was allowed, with my younger brothers, who were all teen-agers, to return home to my father. I had learned to love only books and the natural, physical world of flower, tree, bird, and sky. My big brothers were both married and gone. My father was still silent. That year, I was accepted into college, and the threat of the technical school was gone forever.

I never did become a doctor. In college, all the fragments of my life, the chipped bones of loneliness, of betrayals and schemes for survival, piled up in a mocking skeleton to haunt me. The chaos of early years bloomed, repeated itself in lapses of discipline, fleshing out that skeleton. I had a bad time with drink, and rough affairs with girls. In retrospect, I can see that I was lucky to have got through four years.

I didn't see Ellen from the time I was twelve until I was twenty-one. When I was about fifteen, I learned from the old couple in Rock Point that she had left them abruptly a few years before and had gone house-keeping someplace else; they didn't know where, and I was afraid to make any effort to find out. Then one day, just before leaving home for my senior year of college, I was walking down the main street of our town and I met Ellen's sister, Mabel. She looked exactly as she had the afternoons Ellen had taken me to visit her, with her freckles, rimless glasses, and fading red hair contained in a thick, shimmering hairnet. I remembered the farm vividly and told her so. After the usual polite questions, I asked for Ellen. Mabel said that for the past three years Ellen had been at Laurel Heights. That was a shock. Laurel Heights was a euphemism for the poor-house. I said I was sorry. I didn't know what to add to that. Mabel said that her husband wouldn't let her have Ellen at the farm, because she'd grown so ornery. I said that I would keep in touch with Ellen from now on.

A few days later, I took a walk to the vicinity of the poorhouse. The building sat high on a hill, and I could see the top of it floating above everything. The day was mellow, languorous. Thinking about Ellen, I recalled a narrow-minded, cantankerous, mysterious woman who had loved me as a child and whom I had betrayed. The memory invoked that other September afternoon, and the odor of ripe wild grapes suddenly hung among the ragweed and sumac growing between the low store buildings I was passing.

The huge, brick, columned edifice came into full view. I tried to keep going; I tried to promise myself that I would visit Ellen some other day. But I pumped up the hill, walked along a gravel drive, and went into the building through wide screen doors. I spoke to a nurse. She directed me to the solarium and gave me a bed number. I entered a big room filled with sunlight and the smell of alcohol and urine; two rows of white enamelled-metal beds lined the walls. I went down the wide aisle between them and stopped before the number the nurse had mentioned. There, in a high bed, under a white spread, lay a flat, wide old woman with single-braided gray hair. The familiar mole and warts were on her wrinkled face and neck. Her eyes were closed.

I went up beside her. There was a tall fan buzzing in the corner. Under it, a thin, white-haired man in a blue-and-white striped seersucker robe and white cotton pajamas sat in a maple platform rocker, reading a newspaper with elaborate dignity. I looked at Ellen, pale and still. Gently, I touched her pasty arm, and her eyes opened. They were as black as ever, but watery, and purplish around the rims of the irises. "Ellen?" I said, trembling.

She looked at me with no understanding.

I repeated her name. Then I said, "I'm Terry."

She looked very hard at me. Her brown lips moved. She said in a weak, saliva-clotted voice, "Terry?" She began to cry.

I took her bony hand and held it tight. She squeezed my hand hard, as if she were using all the strength she had.

I thought, This sonofabitching bastard life. I tried to contain myself, to be cheerful. I spoke about the nice weather, and said that it was a nice place and I was sure they were taking good care of her. There was a lot of silence. And then I heard myself saying, "I'm sorry, I couldn't help it, I had to."

She wept again—soundlessly, more intensely. I kept saying, "I'm sorry," but now I meant that I had spoken.

She blew her nose with a tissue I gave her from the metal stand beside her bed. Finally subsiding, she said softly through her gums, "Are you a doctor now?"

I had forgotten that dream two years before. I said not yet but that I was going to college.

She said she was happy, that I'd come a long way. She tried to lift herself closer to me, but couldn't. She said that she was in bed all the time now because her legs had given out from walking all her life. She tried to smooth her hair. As soon as she had her strength back, she said, she'd go to work again.

I heard this as I stood in silence and the fan buzzed, the proud man sat with his paper, someone moaned, someone else babbled. I saw that Ellen was going to sleep. I told her that I was leaving, and that I would come back again when I could to see her. I took her hand and looked at it as I held it. The skin was soft—not as I remembered. I kissed her on the forehead, and when she let go of my hand I walked out, waving stupidly as I went. After the light of the solarium, the hall was dark and cool and blurred.

At Christmastime that year, while I was home on vacation, one evening my father turned from the TV set and said what was for him a volume of words. He spoke in Greek. He said, "Do you remember that woman, Eleni, who used to take care of you when you were small? She died last month—or was it the end of October? Her sister stopped by the store. She said to be sure to tell you Eleni was glad you went to see her in the hospital."

Bright images moved and sounded on the TV screen. I remembered the hot and dusty cemetery where Ellen's mother was. I asked if Mabel had said where Ellen was buried.

My father answered, "She said to tell you, if you asked, 'Potter's Field.'" The words came out in broken English, innocently, as if Potter's Field were a designated locus, a place that could contain the human heart.

In Transit

T HE SOFA SAT in the middle of the living room.
Terry had rolled up the carpet, and it lay long
and limp against a wall. He had disassembled
most of the bookcases—pine boards and yellow bricks
—and packed the books into cardboard boxes. The
boxes were stacked, ready to be taken by the movers at
nine o'clock in the morning. Terry stared at the shiny
hardwood floor. He said, "Laura, you know this floor's
in good shape." His voice was hollow, echoey.

His wife was in the bedroom and did not answer.
He went in to her. In a tight Z shape, she was crouched
close to the floor in the closet. She was cleaning out two
years' worth of old shoes, forgotten dresses, boxes, dead
pocketbooks, faded travel posters, crumpled felt hats,
bent wire coat hangers. She had on an old pair of blue
patterned shorts, a black turtleneck sweater, and sneakers. She never wore such clothes. She had found them
while cleaning and packing. How small and neatly dis-
parate she looked, her beautiful black hair hiding her
face as she leaned forward. She reached and reached,
pulling out more stuff—like entrails—and threw it into
a heap in the middle of the room.

"You know," Terry said, just for the sake of talking, "the floor in the living room is in better shape than
I remembered."

"Mmm." More heavings.

90

The calico bedroom curtains had been taken down. The white walls were bare. There was nothing on the bureau. The pile of debris on the floor and the bed were all that was left in the room. "Laura," Terry said.

She looked up, flushed. Irritation flickered in her dark eyes.

Terry glanced at his watch. Midnight. He shrugged and went back to the living room. It had been stripped of curtains, too. The stereo set was boxed, and records were heaped on the floor. The overhead light glared in all the emptiness. Terry's footsteps were noisy —a lonely sound. He wondered why he should feel lonely. He ought to be excited. This place had been too small. Terry was bony and tall, and he had always been bumping his elbows, tripping over something. He would be glad to get to the new apartment in the city nearby, where he had grown up. The rooms were much larger. He looked out the front window. No shades. Dust everywhere. The main street was empty. Far away, on Long Island Sound, a beacon pulsated. He thought, We *should* move. Too small. Neighbors nosy. Town too little, nothing to do.

He turned. Two more shelves of books, and that would be done; the living room would be finished. Then he would pack whatever china Laura had not packed, and glassware, and anything else he could find. Terry stared at the case of books. Christ, how tired he was of them. What a burden to carry around from place to place for the rest of your life. But he loved books. Laura did, too. They sometimes bought fifteen dollars' worth of paperbacks at a clip, and then complained to friends that they were broke. How many of the books were still unread—yet they were always here, waiting, full of color outside and possibilities inside. They were dependable, unchanging. And they told whatever set of truths and lies one needed to have from them.

Terry went to the kitchen doorway. He shouted, "You want another drink?"

"O.K.," Laura said, her voice muffled. Terry opened the unlit, musty-smelling, defrosted refrigerator, got out a jug of warm orange juice, and poured it into two sticky jelly glasses. From a bottle of vodka he added a large shot to each glass and carried one in to his wife.

Sitting on the floor, she took a sip. "It's awful," she said, "but it helps."

"Too bad there's no vermouth. I could have made Martinis."

"But there's no ice, either, honey." She set the glass down and went back to her foraging.

How could there be so much stuff in such a small closet, Terry wondered. His own closet had a few sports jackets and a couple of suits hanging in it, two or three pairs of shoes on the floor. He took a swallow of his drink. It burned in his stomach and felt good. He threaded his way back to the living room. He glued together a big cardboard box, squatted before the bookcase, pulled out a handful of paperbacks, dusted their tops with an old piece of flannel, and shoved them into one corner of the box. He did the same with another pile. Then, to balance the box, he added three heavy textbooks from the shelf below.

The next book he pulled out made him pause. It was a large, thick one, with a faded orange cover. Its title was printed in a narrow brown circle on the front: "Ingall's Encyclopedic Dictionary and Comprehensive Self-Educator: Multi-pictured Edition." Terry turned a few pages. He stood up, grimaced from the ache in his back, went to the sofa, pushed lampshades, vacuum-cleaner parts, bric-a-brac aside, and sat down.

His first feeling was delight. He had forgotten that the book was still among his possessions—he had not thought of it for years. Laura must have put it on the shelf when they were first married and setting up the apartment. He didn't even remember bringing the book from home. He hefted it. Big as it was, it weighed a trifle. The yellowing paper was cheap, cracking. A stupid book, really. A big, stupid, cheaply made book. How long had he kept it? Twenty years. What a dope. But he had cherished it once. It was from Ellen Slocum, the woman who had taken care of him for two years when he was a boy. His mother had died after a long illness when he was eleven, and in the chaos that followed, his father had got Ellen to come look after him and his two older brothers. An old maid, fifty-six, she was a dishwasher at his father's small restaurant. Before that, she had been a seamstress in local textile mills, but they had all closed and moved South. Through the months that his mother was bedridden, Terry walked to the restaurant from school every noon and ate a hot lunch. He sat up at the counter and made faces and told jokes to Ellen. She laughed until tears came to her eyes as she bent over the stainless-steel sinks full of steaming water and suds and dirty dishes.

When she moved into the apartment, she demanded good behavior. Terry's brothers were teen-agers, used to doing what they wanted. And they resented her taking the place of their mother. Ellen could do nothing with them. For a time, she tried—shouting, cursing at them, getting so angry she wept—and then she let them go. They were wild, free. Terry was wild, too, but much younger. He liked Ellen, with her quirks, her funny high-collared clothes, her odd fits of affection. Though she was often cross, he needed her. She loved him, kept him close to her, tamed him. She took him everywhere with her. She taught him manners. He learned to surrender a little. He obeyed her. The family was poor, and out of her own money she bought him new clothes, a bicycle, games, books. Like this book—this encyclo-

pedia-dictionary thing. Was it the last remnant of Ellen? He could think of nothing else he owned from her.
He would hang on to it. He could still remember the
day she bought it for him.

He was eleven years old. It was raining; he had to
stay in. There was a knock at the door, and Ellen answered. Terry could hear a salesman in the dark hallway
giving her a big pitch about a book. When he heard
Ellen say that she wasn't about to be gypped, he went
out and asked to see it. The salesman quickly held the
book out to Terry. It was opened to a full-color double
page of carrion birds and birds of prey—in the center a
huge, fierce eagle. There was a California condor.
There was a kingfisher, with a fish still struggling in his
cruel beak. Terry said he wished he could have the
book. Ellen stood there—tall, heavy, stiff—in her long
maroon housecoat and flat gray felt slippers. The hard,
dry fingers of one of her hands moved nervously over
the bun of her gray hair. The salesman was bending
over, smiling, breathing heavily. Terry asked again if he
could have the book. Ellen took it from the salesman.
She wet a finger on her tongue and turned pages. Terry
knew she could not comprehend what she was looking
at. She was half blind from years of close work at the
mills. He was always threading needles for her; it took
her hours to read the newspaper at night under a bright
lamp. "How much is it?" she said, her purplish lips
forming a tight Yankee line. When the salesman told
her, she said it was too much. "Please," Terry said, and
he squeezed her rough hand. She looked down at him
and her eyes softened. "All right," she said with disgust.
She paid the man out of a little leather change purse
that snapped at the top.

Terry read in that book for hours. Days. It was
one of the first adult books that made him want other

books. It was full of knowledge, most of it useless to a boy. It had a gold-colored thumb index: Business-law dictionary; Medical dictionary; Pictorial self-educator; Office worker's guide; Synonyms and antonyms; Atlas and gazetteer; A cyclopedia of nature. That last section was on slick paper, and it had captivated him. Terry opened the book to it now. In full color, hundreds of species of living things moved among designs of leaves. There were pages of butterflies and moths. North American insects. American game fish, floating together, dropping one against the other, swimming in every direction, with their common names beside them printed neatly among the seaweed and blue-green water. Song and perching birds—Terry had spent a lot of time drawing them, soaking up their colors. There were wild North American fur-bearing animals. North American reptiles—fearsome, coiled, with bared fangs. Some snakes surrounded piles of eggs. The coral snake looked particularly beautiful and deadly. There were conifers, flowering trees and shrubs, wild flowers, and garden flowers—vivid even after all these years. Mushrooms flared, with a small printed warning about those that were poisonous. American desert plants bloomed.

Terry closed the dictionary, put it on the sofa, and shut his eyes. It had been a strange, lonely time. Ellen, strange and lonely herself, had been good to him, and he had loved her. If he thought about her, he would never finish tonight. He got up, returned to packing the rest of the books. He separated the shelves and bricks. He went to the kitchen, made another drink, and took a long draught. Besides depression from so much disorder, he felt a deep melancholy.

It was one-fifteen in the morning. He was packing china and glass. Slowly, he wrapped the delicate pieces in newspaper and placed them carefully in boxes. A roaring noise came from the bedroom. Laura was vacuuming. The two of them were half insane now with fatigue, and half drunk, and full of dust.

The orange juice was gone. Terry poured a straight shot of vodka into his glass and finished it off in a swallow. He took another swig directly from the bottle. It tasted bitter, and stung his tongue. "Laura," he shouted above the noise. He went to her.

She said, "I've got to finish this." She looked desperate. Her hair was full of cobwebs. Her eyes were heavy, red, and teary from the dust.

He hugged her and said, "What's wrong with me? I don't want to move. It would have been O.K. here for a while, until we began to have a family."

"You're tired," she said. "The books were crowding us out. You said so yourself. You'll feel better when we get into the new place." She touched his face and went on with her work.

She was so calm, steady. He loved her for it. He thought she would transmit her serenity to him. He stood there. Soon the vacuum tank was a brown beaver, its hose a striped snake. That book—that stupid picture dictionary. He got it from the sofa and brought it to Laura. He shouted, "You remember this book? You remember I told you about that woman who took care of me when I was little and gave it to me?"

Laura nodded, banging the vacuum hose under the bed. She looked at him wearily.

"You think I should keep it?"

"What?" Laura turned off the machine.

"I think I'll throw it out," Terry said. His voice boomed. "It's just a cheap goddam book with a lot of useless stuff in it."

"Keep it," Laura said. "You've always spoken fondly of her." She turned on the machine.

Terry went to the kitchen and put the book on

the table. Slowly, he stacked pots and pans in bushel baskets. He looked at the book. "I don't want it," he mumbled. The place was a wreck. It was two o'clock. Trash was crawling away from the sink toward the center of the kitchen. Terry opened the back door and, making several trips, carried all the trash to the porch. He got the book from the table, went outside, took the lid off the garbage pail. The smell of orange peel and coffee grounds rose up strong. He pushed down with his hand to make space and put the book on top. He replaced the lid and went back into the kitchen.

Now he was stuffing all the cleaning things—cans, boxes, jars, bottles—from under the sink into a carton. Suddenly he noticed that the bedroom was silent. He looked in. Laura lay asleep, uncovered on the bed directly under the bright ceiling light. Pale, with dirty, curled hands, her mouth slightly open, she looked like a small, helpless child. Gently, he shook her awake. "Take off your clothes and get into bed," he said. "We'll finish whatever there is early in the morning." He set the alarm for seven. Laura dragged herself up and obeyed. Terry turned off the light. He felt lightheaded, weak. Automatically, he went back to more packing: the medicine chest, the top shelf in the pantry, with its accumulation of tools, wire, clothespins, paper bags. Finally, he could do no more work. He drank what was left of the vodka.

He took off just his shoes and socks and lay on the bed. He did not even think of sleep. It would come without effort.

But sleep did not come. Even the liquor didn't help. Boxes, dishes, clothes, trash, the vacuum cleaner, rows of books marched by. He bent down, lifted, tied it all up. The motions occurred rhythmically in his mind, over and over. And then the thick, faded orange encyclopedia floated before him in the dark, its pages open, all the colors blurring—fish and fowl, tree and flower. Ellen. She had died ten years before—alone, forgotten —in the poorhouse. By now she was dust. Who would remember her?

Terry got up and stumbled against boxes stacked in the dark. He unlocked the back door and went out to the porch in his bare feet. It was a chilly, black night, soundless. He had not noticed before. Leaning over the rail, turning his head, he could just see the stars—faint, constant—and he was grateful for them.

He straightened up, took the cover off the garbage pail. Metal moving on metal shrieked in the dewy silence. Terry felt inside the pail. The book was still there on top, flat and cold, hard. He went to lift it out. Something held him back. He paused in the huge darkness. Very slowly, lovingly, he moved the palm of his hand over the damp book cover. He left the book where it was and replaced the lid of the pail.

Back in the apartment, he felt his way to the bedroom, took off his clothes, and got into bed. He curled up close to the warmth of Laura's body. She lay still, breathing deeply, evenly. He wanted so much to say something. But what could he tell anyone—even her? After a while, he fell asleep.

Fathers

MY MOTHER, flicking a piece of gray hair out of her eyes, puts a big platter of sandwiches in the center of the table. She mumbles, glowers at Dad, who has just now, at five o'clock, come home from the V.F.W. bar. Breathing hard, he stuffs the salami and tomatoes and bread into his mouth. He laughs a little. He burps, loud.

"Timothy McPhale!" Mom says, scowling.

"Hmm, hmm," he sings. His blue eyes are watery.

My sister Catherine says, "Next he'll give us a chorus of 'My Wild Irish Rose.'"

"Now *you* be quiet," says Mom.

I look at my wife, Chloe. My wild Grecian rose, I think, laughing. She sits beside me, her black hair straight and parted in the middle. My four-month bride, who is pregnant now, and I, side by side. She nibbles silently, full of good manners in her red wool dress. I put my foot on hers under the table. She tries a weak smile.

My brother Tommy looks across at me with his sly hazel eyes like Mom's, then secretly at Dad, then back at me. "Hey Joey, you know what?" he says to me, grinning. He is a small fox with freckles. My wife's leg touches mine gently. The kitchen is bright, with light-green walls, blue curtains, the brown walnut table. There are scattered branches of holly on the bench by the stove, waiting for Catherine to make them into decorations. Tommy says, "I made the Boys' League basketball team."

"Yah, just," says Dad.

"What do you mean?"

"Well, you just got under the line, didn't you? For the twelve-year-olds."

"Oh."

"No, I wasn't meaning about whether you was good or not."

"He *has* to be good," I say. "He has to be a star like his father was."

My father's eyes connect with mine for an instant. I look at Mom. Old family rhythms. Her eyes are yellowish, somewhat the color of a goat's, I think. And to myself I say, "No, Father, I didn't mean it in a rotten way, honestly." I should say it out loud. I should look right into those beery eyes and say, "Father, you *were* a great star, you're a legend. Everyone knows. I'm proud of you. Goddamit, I mean it."

Outside, the sun fades over the lonely hills. "He was, he was," I say to Chloe.

Everyone fidgets. Mom gets up and pours the coffee. Catherine sidles from thigh to thigh in her chair, eating her big sandwich. Daddy slaps her on the arm. "My Kate," he says. She is big, like him.

Do the genes know, I wonder. Have they plans in their spiralled darkness? My sister Catherine, for all that she is pink and demurely clever, even feminine, might have been a great halfback. Whereas I shivered through some fifteen years of gymnasium. I was always aware of high, glittering slants of dust, the smell of varnish that made me feel somehow secure, the funny shape of my sneakers, the itchy feel of my white wool socks; I gazed at ceilings of braces and joists, at twining networks of black-painted steel, at latticed windows full of morning light; I heard confusing shouts around me. And I moved up and down the courts like a grocery cart. I never felt the heat and obsession of the game. No, I never did.

I say to myself, "Tell him, now, though he ignores you."

But he knows. He said once, pointing with a log of a forefinger to his giant head of white hair, "When you've got it up here, you don't have to worry, lad." Did he mean it? Didn't he burn to toss a football with me out in the yard, to cheer me on to bat a stinging hard ball over the fence? And now, with Tommy, he's too old, he's too fat, too tired.

Dad is the first finished eating. Leaning on the table, hoisting it a bit with his weight, he elbows Tommy, winks. Tommy smiles with a rapturous shyness. "Do you understand each other?" I want to say. Tommy, too, disappears in books by the hour, as I did. He is reading Kipling, enjoying tales of blood and courage.

"Timothy, sit up, for goodness' sakes!" Mom says. Twenty-five years of his drinking. Her plump face reddens.

He doesn't look at her, but, like a child, obeys.

"You and your late Mass," she says. "Mass" hisses. Every Sunday after church, my father—for how many years now?—spends his afternoons at the V.F.W. with cronies and TV football games. He comes home puffing, his color jaundiced. I think, Who are you running away from? Oh, Dad, take care of yourself.

"Chloe, would you care for more coffee?" Mom says.

"No, thank you, Mrs. McPhale." Chloe is tense; I can feel it in her leg next to mine.

"All right. Out now, everyone," Mom says. "I have to clean up here."

"I'll help," Chloe says, her pale round face flushed.

"No, you rest, dear. It's easy to lose it in the third month." She gives orders, scoops up cups and saucers, Chloe helping her anyway.

Dad rises, unloads himself into the living room. In a minute, he is asleep in his chair. The TV glows with a rerun of the afternoon football game. Tommy is curled in the semi-dark with his Kipling. Catherine is doing her Latin homework at the dining-room table. My wife and mother are washing the dishes.

There is no sound, only a whirl—a visual imprint on my brain—as I float in the doorway watching my father for a long time. I see a giant asleep, sprawled, his white shirt stretched taut across his belly. I am balanced dangerously on a long filament that has no end. I walk here slowly, painfully, putting one narrow foot forward and then the other, swaying. My arms are out straight on either side of me. Everything rushes. Just when I think, Help! I'm falling, I see him down there all alone and I'm saved.

There are goodbyes that seem soundless. Mom gives Chloe a piece of Christmas fruitcake wrapped in aluminum foil. It is all like a dream.

Outside, sound rushes, finally, in wind and the cracking of icy tree trunks.

We drive six blocks to Chloe's house. "Let's not stay long, please," she begs, as if I would keep her. We pull into the drive of the shadowed house with the big maple creaking out front. The place is totally dark, but we know she's in there. We go through the kitchen, and up the stairs to her room.

Chloe snaps on the light. Her mother squints—pained—shields her eyes, which are as black as my wife's. Promise me, Chloe, that won't ever be you, I am thinking.

"Hello, Mother," Chloe says, and bends her slender body down to the short chubby woman sitting on the bed in a red sweater and a blue print housedress, cotton stockings, men's brown leather slippers. She has brooches all over the front of her sweater—zircon and glass, brass and fake pearls—and two St. Christopher medals and a gold cross on a safety pin attached to the dress at her throat. Her hands are as little as a child's, her hair black, her nose straight. She must have been beautiful once.

Chloe talks to her in Greek. My mother-in-law understands English but refuses to speak it.

"Tell me, too," I want to say.

Then Chloe speaks. "She says it's cold in her room at night. You know, this always was a cold little room."

Her mother talks again.

"She says she's hungry, that Father locks away the food, gives her only a drop at a time. But you know he has to." And Chloe recites for the twentieth time, "It's the only way he can keep her alive. Otherwise, she'd eat herself to d-e-a-t-h." The concept of death is refused by her mother, and she gets upset if it is mentioned in her presence. She says she is going to live forever.

Now she is speaking again. "What?" I say.

"The same old thing. That he wasn't always like this. That he was wonderful to her once. But he changed. She says he has a woman. That he stays out gambling in the Greek coffeehouse half the night. She's been saying it for years. And he *was* nice to her—even I remember. And to me, too, when I was very little. But I don't believe it about the other woman. We never heard anything all this time, and I'm sure we would have, somehow. There's always some witch to tell that kind of tale."

Her mother is playing with her hands.

"Give her some fruitcake," I say. "The poor creature."

"She says she is not a poor creature."

We all smile.

Chloe opens the foil, breaks off a piece of cake, offers it. Her mother takes it into her pink hands and, like a rat, puts it to her drawn-down mouth.

Chloe turns her eyes to me. I look out the uncurtained, black, glittering pane. The wind moves a thin lace of branches very close to the house.

Chloe strokes her mother's hair. "Mommy," she says in English, "you know what? I'm going to have a baby."

Her mother stops chewing for an instant. She looks first at Chloe, then at me, with eyes that have no pupils visible and therefore no expression. She stares at the piece of cake, chews again, slowly.

Chloe repeats in Greek.

"*Alétheia?*" says her mother.

I know that means "truth."

"Yes," Chloe says, her back straightening, tall.

Looking down at her slippers, my mother-in-law moves her mouthful of food a little more. At last, she raises her eyes to her daughter. An open smile cracks her face. Her eyes seem to have lit somewhat.

"In June," Chloe says.

Her mother speaks.

Chloe translates. "She says, 'Good, the baby will be healthy. Won't have the colds that winter babies do.'"

More Greek from her mother.

"I don't know exactly how to translate it," Chloe says. "It's a wish, a greeting. Literally, it's 'May it live for you.' '*Na sas zísi.*' The child. She wishes it life for us. It's a Greek salutation and hope. You say it at christenings, and you say it to the bride's and groom's parents at Greek weddings, only in the plural: 'May they live for you.' " Chloe says to her mother, "Was anyone here today?"

"No."

She looks at her mother intently. "What about Father? Was Father here?"

Her mother answers coldly.

"She says, 'That stranger who lives here? He was in this afternoon to take a nap.' He must have come home from work for a while."

Chloe turns up one of the sleeves of her mother's sweater, smoothes it. She says, "Mama, will you tell him? Tell him that I'm going to have a *baby*."

Her mother says nothing. She shakes her head slightly, no.

"Yes. Tell him. He's my father."

Her father. He didn't even come to our wedding. "But don't you understand?" Chloe had said. "He didn't come because of the Catholic Church. He said he never wants to see me again." Then she explained about religion and nationality being inseparably bound together for all Greeks who had come across, all the people her family had known when she was a little girl in the tenement and her mother was all right, when the ladies used to visit back and forth. "Marry nize Greek boy" was all that Chloe had ever heard. But she married me. Quickly, with no Mass, in the chilly church of my childhood one morning in September. Her father did not come at all. His place at the wedding breakfast afterward was empty. All of my family surrounded us. But her mother sat beside me; Chloe had seen to her coming. Struggling into a silk flowered dress, with Chloe helping her early in the morning, her mother had said, "Church? What difference does it make what church, as long as you are kind to each other?" Would she have said the same thing if she had been well? Anyway, she sat next to her husband's empty plate, unconscious of everyone and everything except food, as she stuffed herself with muffins and eggs and bacon and ham and jam (spooning it into her mouth right out of the jam pot) and champagne, not saying a word. And Chloe, upset, squeezing my hand, said to me in the plush rooms of the inn where the small reception was held, "Try to understand. He can't help it. He has his pride." I wanted to say, "Well, I have mine, too," but I kept quiet.

Chloe is leaning over her mother. "Please tell him," she says. "You *have* to tell him."

Her mother finishes the piece of cake. I feel restless. In the long quiet that follows, I am lulled by the wind outside. I stare at the bureau next to me. Its top is loaded with faded birthday cards; pink ribbon; Christmas wrapping paper—used, full of dust; folded paper luncheon napkins; pins; a three-year-old calendar with a picture of two Scotty dogs on it; two unused tea bags rolled together; a gaudy, large, somehow lovely cheap icon print.

Chloe thrusts the remaining piece of foil-wrapped cake into her mother's hands. "Come on, please, let's go," she says to me. "Goodbye, Mommy," she says, touching one of the four or five brooches. It glints. "Don't turn the light off, will you, Mama. Leave it on. It's not nice to be in the dark. It's not pleasant."

Her mother nods again, agreeing with her, childlike, holding on tight to her crumpled silvery parcel.

"Goodbye. We'll come again soon. You'll have to come out to our place where we live now. It's not far from town. We'll come and get you. You can have dinner with us. You'd like that, wouldn't you? Soon. Goodbye, dear."

Getting into the car, I say, "What made him change?"

Chloe says, "How can we ever know who changed first."

In the moving car, I look back just in time to see the bar of light that is her mother's room turn to sudden darkness.

We race through town. It is already deserted at nine o'clock. To get to the highway, we ride down the main streets of closed shops. We glide under ropes of laurel twined with colored lights.

As we pass a darkened drugstore Chloe's hand goes up in a jerk. "Oh," she says.

"What?"

"That was my father's car parked. He's upstairs, then, in the Greek coffeehouse."

The dirty bastard, I think, and almost say it.

My wife says, "The poor creature."

Ahead, there's a small Italian grocery store that's still open. "Do we need any damn bread?" I ask. "Or milk or anything?"

"No. I just want to go home. I don't feel well."

"It's the baby, darling," I say. "I'm sorry." And I think, Please, baby, be a son and have my father's strength and Tommy's Kipling, and your mother's eyes and gentleness.

I look at Chloe. By now the tears are standing in her eyes, ready to spill.

"He'll be a cynical girl," I say out loud. "He'll have a mustache and wear dresses and ride a boy's bike and embroider and turn mad and silent at the end."

Chloe frowns questioningly, tilts her head at me, then lays it softly on my shoulder. I look quickly, see the tears slide. She says nothing, my mysterious wife.

We rush out of the town under thick garlands of fresh Nativity greens swinging above the empty streets.

A Lecture

LATE ONE APRIL AFTERNOON, Uncle Panos sat across from Mike in Mike's brother's restaurant. He said in his gravelly voice, "How you can live these way? How old you are now?"

"I was twenty-seven last month."

"Almost thirty. Nice-looking boy. Not married, no respo'sibilities, useless. Like failure."

His moist brown eyes were set deep among brown wrinkles. His hair was very gray. One day soon he'll die, Mike thought, looking at him. Poof. Heart. Like Uncle Costas, who died last Easter. Dyed red eggs inside his casket along with the cheap icon. Seven dollars and eighty-five cents in his pants' pockets. All he had. Alone, in a veterans' hospital in New Haven. His family back in Albania, inaccessible. But he was a gay blade. He was *capable* of dying alone. Mike stared at his uncle's eyes, and he thought, Your family is still back there, too. I saw you crying at my brother's wedding. When the nuptial crowns were exchanged, you were thinking of your son's wedding you never went to, of grandchildren you'll never see.

"What becomes of you?" Uncle Panos said. "How you can ever have home, new car—what's that piece junk you driving, aren't you shamed youself, college-educated boy? What happen to the smart boy you was? And you getting skinny, too."

Uncle Panos was smoking. His fingers were permanently rich golden brown with nicotine. His fingernails were thick, corrugated, and yellow. Jesus, Mike thought, what bulky hands he has. From forty years of lifting fruit crates, boxes, cutting his hands, sweating. Now he coughs and splutters, his lungs filling more and more each year. Why? What for?

"You got to organize you life, shame on you. Don't you know people start to talk? The Greek community?" He mouthed the last word. It must have been a new one.

"Who?"

"Not to mention names—names not important."

"Like Vasili Bouros?"

"Well, yes, boy. Yes." Uncle Panos shrugged.

"That pig." Mike ran his fingers rapidly through his thick black hair.

"Now aren't you really shamed youself? He comes here five years ago, stupid, no money, no understanding to the language, and now lookit—he has big frozen-custard stand, home, nice new car. Worth forty thousand."

"He's a pig," Mike said. "My father sponsored him to get into this country. He lived in our house—slept in my bed while I slept on a cot out in the hall. My father gave him a job, and when the rest of Vasili's family came over and they moved into their own apartment he gave them furniture, and clothes, too, and now they never even come to see us. Never. They don't even know us. You think I need him or want to be like him? I'd starve first."

"Just the same. You smart, educated boy. *Now* look, *he* got everything."

"*Everything.* Nothing!"

"Don't talk foolish. These talk you have don't mean nothing. Look. I don't yell to you. I'm talking to you now gentlemen. I'm interesting what you going to be, what you do with you life. All right. You had it good job—hundred dollars a week. You leave it, went like a gypsy in Europe. Now since you come back, lousy jobs, old car—"

"I love that car. My '48 Chevy."

"Bah! Talk sense. And money. For really, now, what you make in that hospital?"

"A dollar an hour."

"Part-time, at night, cleaning from sick old people, you father tell me. He can' do nothing with you, he say. Jesus, boy. Aren't you shamed youself?"

"No."

Uncle Panos' face got red. He sneered. "Why, I come here with nothing—not one goddam penny—work hard, kill myself forty years, save money."

"Now you have it all in the bank, you have your apartment houses, you live in one of them all alone, you are happy, Uncle Panos."

"Tell me," he said. "What *is* these thing you are doing?"

"But you know, Uncle. Everyone tells you about your brother's lazy son." Mike sighed. "Reading. Learning." It would have been suicide to mention that he was trying to write poems.

Uncle Panos pressed his lips together, turned them down at the corners, nodded shortly, and said, "The Great Philosopher," in Greek. He went on in broken English, "What, you can' do these on the side? Get good job again in the office you was in and do these study part-time?"

"Good job? Part-time? I have my honor," Mike said, smiling.

Uncle Panos groaned. His dark fat face twitched.

"Honor? You remind it me of lawyer in the old country. These one time, he wouldn't take a case. No honesty in it, he say to me. And he talk about *his* honor. Baloney. He was poor, never marry because of his honor." The aspirate "h"s fell thick and heavily Greek. "You gonna be half rooster, too, like we say, with no wife and kids?"

Mike wanted to say to him, "Why not? You are. When it was still possible to get your wife and kids out of Albania and bring them here, you didn't." But he kept his mouth shut out of an old, learned respect. "I'm going to die like my Uncle Costas—alone and single," he said.

"Don't talk like these." Uncle Panos frowned. "He was big fool."

"Because he didn't care about making a fortune in America? And gambled what he had on the horses and drank himself to death and made fun of the rest of you? That's why he was a fool? He was the only free one of all of you who came over together." Mike got ready to leave. He had had enough of listening to his uncle, of sitting in the red plastic booth, looking at the variegated plastic tropical plants in a long green plastic box on a formica sideboard.

Just then his brother George came to work. He was thirty-four, dark-haired, and handsome. He was quiet, like their father. As he walked behind the counter, he hardly said hello. His eyes were puffy from a late-afternoon sleep. He had the night shift this month.

"Why you can' be like him?" Uncle Panos said.

"Because I don't want to be like him. *He's* lost, not me."

"He's make it lotta money, married, got two kids, insurance business on the side. He be worth plenty some day."

"I wish him good luck. Him and all his damn

money," Mike said. And he thought, Behind my back, they all shake their heads. "Lost." They put their hands to their mouths and tell one another in Greek.

"I tell you for you own good," Uncle Panos said.

"*Your* own good. My own evil."

"Talk plain."

"Plain I talk."

"O.K., now you make it fun of me."

"No. You make fun of *me*," Mike said.

Uncle Panos raised his shoulders. Then he leaned forward, opened his big hands in front of him, and said imploringly, "What you want to *be*? What you care about?"

"What I care about." Mike looked across the restaurant, out the window, up Main Street. He talked rapidly. "Let me tell you what I care about. A little while ago, before I came in to eat, I was walking up the street. It was cloudy out. The world felt restless. I looked up and saw a mystery. You know what it was? Rain. A spring shower. I saw it move, very slowly, right down the street toward me, coming long and thin, silvery. Gliding. Not hurting anything. Just splitting the late afternoon—understand? Delicate. Then it got to me and it touched me with gentleness, and it didn't ask for anything in return. It didn't ask for a cent. I was in front of the bookstore. . . . Wait. Don't get up. Listen. I just by luck happened to get caught in the rain in front of a bookstore. I went in and looked at books for over an hour—you hear? No one asked for pay, and no one paid me for my time. I looked at every kind of book. And other people wandered around in there, too, and no one said anything. No one made any kind of a demand. No one told me to go out and earn forty thousand dollars or asked me why I'm wasting my life."

Uncle Panos got up. "You get out of the rain, anyways. Maybe you be all right still."

Mike held back his uncle's heavy wrist. "Please. Let me finish. There were all kinds of books, all colors and sizes—rough and smooth, cheap, expensive. I read in some of them, standing there, and I could smell the print, the beautiful chemicals of the ink."

Uncle Panos stood squat and proud, important, wonderful in his old ballooning brown gabardine pants. His head was erect, his chest fat and marvellous, his chin pulled in making two or three chins. His brand of English fell handsome from his loose-hanging lips. "Well, I don't know one word of all these you are talking. Poor fool. Half rooster. *Honor.* Bah! Someday, is true, you *really* die like you uncle, you mother's tragedy fool of a brother." Greek fashion, he mock-spat at Mike, but without malice.

Mike smiled. Uncle Panos put his whole hand over Mike's head and tousled his hair, giving him a kindly peasant benediction, as though Mike were ten years old again. Then Uncle Panos strutted toward George, who was putting on a clean starched white apron as he stood by the coffee urns. They talked together.

Mike sat alone for a while. He stared out the window, remembering the warm rain and the bittersweet smell of all the new books.

Now he felt the waitress hanging over him like a fly on a summer day. He got up and put a quarter on the table. She grinned, gap-toothed, and said, "Thanks!" as she began to swab the table.

Mike put on his coat. He went to the counter and gave George his check, with a dollar for the food. George pushed the dollar back to his brother and folded the check. "I'll take care of it," he said. He slipped the check into the pocket of his fresh white shirt. This was not the first time George had kept a check, but Mike had never really thought about it before. He looked down at the tile floor until its stark black-and-white tiny squares hurt his eyes. When he finally looked up, Uncle Panos was staring at him, grinning.

George said to Mike, "He giving you some trouble?"

"A lecture," Mike said, flushed.

George looked content, innocent, full of peace. With his soft brown eyes, he was sleek and beautiful, and he seemed, as always, to enjoy the role of big brother.

"Any new deals?" Mike said. He knew that George loved that question.

"I got a big new apartment house in the works— comprehensive, full commission," he said. He talked softly, out of the side of his mouth. "Keep it under your hat."

"Good," Mike said. He motioned toward his uncle and said, "I was telling him that I'm going to die just like Uncle Costas."

George chuckled. Uncle Panos grunted, smiled painfully, and called Mike a stupid son of a bitch. Mike started out the door.

"Where you going?" George asked.

"Nowhere," Mike said.

George shook his head and touched his shirt pocket.

Mike went out. He walked up Main Street in the twilight full of moving pedestrians and cars. The shower had gone by long ago. The air was chilly. In the sky the clouds were breaking and racing south, a huge red sun setting ragged among them. He walked past the bookstore. All the street lights suddenly went on together, glazing the wet sidewalks and the wet macadam street, but there was no mystery.

The Empire of Things

WE WALKED THROUGH the vast Tudor building. There were many of us registering. I was surprised and happy to see college friends from ten years ago whom I had not seen since graduation. Don Fielding came in. His face was red and shiny, and he had all of his hair; he looked exactly as he had in first-year French; only a class beanie was lacking. "What are you doing here?" I asked him. Shyly, he pulled at his crew-neck sweater and said, "The same thing you are."

We shuffled through a long line. Trembling little old women gave us our clothes and gear. At the end of the first line, a fat woman handed me a folded green entrenching tool. "You must be careful of color and concealment," she said. I looked at her closely. She was my elementary-school physical-education teacher—Miss Holstein. Her face was very tan. There was no lipstick on her mouth. She had short, fuzzy brown hair and bowling-pin legs, and she wore a plain mauve suit and pale calfskin flat shoes with thick soles. She held a big brown rubber dodge ball in her left hand.

I started to acknowledge her. She raised a finger

and frowned. I moved on to another line. One of my best friends from college, Tim O'Connell, came in through a dark-stained door full of tiny glittering windowpanes. We embraced and shook hands. He, too, had not changed. He was huge and burly as always, and his laughter was exactly as I remembered it—deep, throaty, almost mournful. He had a large mouth.

I said, "You look the same after all this time."

"So do you," he said. "You haven't changed a bit."

"But I'd have thought everyone would look older."

He shrugged. "How's your family?"

"Great. I miss them. Especially my son. He's seven. The last time I saw him, he was boarding a big yellow school bus on the hill in front of our house. I'd just turned to get into my car when I saw the red signals of the bus flashing. It was raining, and Charlie—that's my son—was the last one on, because he was having trouble closing his umbrella. It was a red umbrella. He's so little I wondered if he was ever going to get it down, but he finally did. I waved with my briefcase, he waved back, and the bus shut off its signals and chugged up the hill. That's the last I saw of him. The rascal."

The huge room, nostalgically like my college dining hall, bustled with men getting their packs together. Someone blew a whistle. Milling and chatting, we settled on the floor. How odd. Now it was kindergarten, with narrow planks beneath us, shiny oak, and we were very close to earth, to the bottom. Would there be a piano and singing? Or cutout time, and furtive eating of paste that tasted of wintergreen?

Miss Holstein came to the front. We stood. She pulled down a silvery granulated screen. There was a flag behind her. We pledged allegiance, sang "God Bless America," and sat down again. With pointer in hand, she said softly, "I am going to give a very brief orientation. Then we will go into the warehouse."

As she talked slowly on and on, the sun shone on her tan, fuzzy face. How much it was like the sun of childhood autumns, early Septembers, when school started. ". . . here to help the troops," she was saying. "We are brave little soldiers in our own way." There was a squirming around me. "Soldiers of mercy. Soldiers of peace, dealing with *things*. We are going to help our fighting men not with prayer, not with entertainment, not even with coffee and doughnuts, but with concrete things that will remind them of home, and civilization, and history, and meaning. Things that will boost our men's morale and help them see it through. Do you understand?"

We all droned peacefully.

"Pull the shades. First slide, please." The windows became deep, warm yellow, the room pleasantly dark. Several maps flashed onto the screen. They showed crude road lines, supply lines, chow areas, latrine areas, the combat zone. Company headquarters—our location —lay on the west. From it three fat black arrows flared north, east, and south. Miss Holstein swept the pointer over the arrows. She said, "This part of the jungle is your working radius. You will use compasses. Next slide, please. Ah. Here are some of the things." Slides flashed in rapid succession. They showed small articles of furniture, glassware, china, toys, linen. The slides ended.

We were taken to an adjoining room, the warehouse. It turned out to be an immaculate museum, with much the same kind of things we had seen on the screen. Each was encased in glass and labelled. "Chippendale chair." "Porringer, 1784." "Hand mirror of Mme. Pompadour." "Earrings from Knossos, 1600 B.C." Stuff like that. We were all impressed.

Miss Holstein gathered us around like a large

group of tourists. Pointing, she said, "When you go through that door, you'll be on your own. Remember to gather your things compactly in a container you'll find, such as a chest or a bureau. And don't take more than you can carry alone. By the time you fill your containers, you should be near enough the combat zone to deliver them personally to our fighting men. Then your mission is done. You will return here. It'll be cookies and milk and a long rest. You'll have earned it. Good luck."

We applauded respectfully. She marched to the door and opened it. Everyone filed through.

The jungle was like home—the woods in New Hampshire. I did not understand. Maple trees, birch, oak, beech, pines. Some swamp. Rocks. But no open fields.

We spread out to find containers for our things. It was fun—like a large Easter-egg hunt. We discovered dust-covered chests; spider-webbed bathtubs with claw feet; old, discarded refrigerators with no doors; abandoned automobiles, upholstery coming out of the seats; huge Victorian trunks. Everything was hidden among bushes, under trees, behind boulders. My colleagues cheered as they found suitable containers. Tim O'Connell was using a baby-blue Volkswagen with no wheels and no engine.

I am not a big man. I chose a strange combination of small bureau and chest. I had never seen such a piece of furniture, so I did not know the name of it. I called it a trunk. It had six big brass handles—three on each long side. Drawers with cut-glass knobs pulled magically out of the narrow ends. Yet the top opened like a lid, and inside there was no sign of the drawers. It was roomy, and you could store a lot in it if you were eclectic and not greedy for large, ostentatious things.

All the men had chosen containers. One picked a

1940-vintage washing machine. It had a small black rubber knob that you turned to let out the water. A stick to stop the agitator. No hose. As I walked by, I peeked in; the large, propeller-like agitator was still in place. I wondered how he expected to fit much in it at all.

Everyone moved out smartly with his empty container. I dragged mine for a while, then shouldered it. It got heavier and heavier. How rapidly we tire, I thought. How frail we are.

When we reached the first large cache, we shouted, "Hurrah!" Men put down their containers and began to scoop up things. We gathered glittering identification necklaces from the green-leaved trees. Sunlight made the quick-moving men shimmer. I stopped. Was it innocence I saw on their faces? The jungle was filled with a shadowy, dappled glow and the sneaky, lithe movements of small boys. Who were the Indians, I wondered. The cowboys. Who were the bad guys and who were the good? I plucked two splendid ruby earrings from a bush where they were hanging and laid them carefully in the flowered fabric bottom of my trunk. No. They would be lost there. They were too small. I put them in one of the small end drawers instead. The drawer was lined with maroon-and-écru striped silk. It smelled of old perfume, talcum powder. Ephemera. Death. I shook my head.

I found a tortoiseshell comb, a satinwood natural-bristle brush. I wondered whose they had been as I laid them gently in the drawer. A bag of marbles, with "Joe—1876" embroidered on it. A First World War lead soldier. He had a pink painted face and a brilliant red dot of a mouth.

I spotted a large, beautiful white porcelain Cheshire cat. I must have dragged the trunk a mile farther before I found some burlap, wrapped the cat up, and put him in the bottom of the sweet-sour trunk. Next to a

tree stump, I found a long leather change purse divided
into two compartments, with two snap prongs to open
and close it. It smelled wonderfully of leather, slightly
moldy. Someone could use it. I put it in one of the
drawers. This drawer was lined with an old yellowed
newspaper. The visible headlines were about a Senate
debate, a stock-market decline, and an accidental
drowning. I came on two hurricane lamps tangled in
brambles. They would do to light a soldier's reading
and correspondence. I wrapped the lamps in many
green leaves and placed them gently in the trunk.

I heard a bullet zing. Must be getting near the
front line. Act fast, I told myself, but choose. Here was a
hobby-horse with one of its madly staring agate eyes
missing. Painted spots on its rippling body were fading,
gone. I wanted to take that, but I had to be selective.
Beside it stood a squat black iron play stove. Charming
but useless. A pair of opera glasses. Perfect for recon-
naissance. Into the trunk with them. Seven home-knit-
ted green woolen mufflers. Four sealed pints of brown,
coagulated Red Cross blood dated January, 1944.
Good.

The mosquitoes were intolerable. It was getting
hotter. Creatures were screaming and moving in the
brush. I found a toy drum. That would do. For signals,
maybe. But it dissolved when I picked it up—rust. Suddenly Tim O'Connell was in front of me. He had taken
off all his clothes. He was hairy and laughable, his beer
belly hanging out. With palette in one hand and brush
in the other, he was painting his baby-blue Volkswagen
khaki and brown, green and black, beige and gray, in
patches like pieces of a jigsaw puzzle.

"Miss Holstein," he said. "Concealment."

I went on, dragging my trunk. As I passed, I
looked at what he had in his Volkswagen. An enormous
clear-plastic bag of popcorn. An elaborate Telefunken

radio. Several red-and-black plaid blankets. An embalming kit. An old, mineral-stained porcelain toilet bowl. About ten pairs of ladies' high-heel pumps, an ostrich boa, and a large goldfish bowl full of packs of prophylactics. A sawhorse, and two stuffed baby alligators. Not very selective, I thought. Yet I must not judge. "I'll see you later," I said. "That's quite a fine collection of things."

"Thanks."

I heaved my trunk onto my back. The terrain was changing. There were vines. Huge tropical flowers. Sweet-smelling, rotting fruit underfoot, and elephant droppings. Monkeys swinging, screeching. Screaming parrots, birds of paradise. Sweat. Flies. The roar of a tiger? You could not be certain. I was groaning under the load of my trunk. God help us, I thought. I heard someone thrashing nearby (cutting with machetes?), and voices. "A thirteenth-century triptych!" "Gramophones!" "Spanish armor!" Squeals of delight.

I wandered frantically. For a while, I could find no things. I was lost. The needle of my compass spun and spun. I just missed a quicksand pit. A nearly endless python slithered past. I walked for a long time.

All at once I was in a dark, misty paradise of things. I could hear no one. The others had gone. I began to gather the things as swiftly as I could, shoving them into drawers, into the trunk. It became a hungry mouth. Rain was threatening. I worked fast. I put in a dozen candlewick cutters and snuffers—silver. Sixteen morning suits, complete with striped cravats. Two beautiful heavy green-and-white croquet mallets, six croquet balls. From a tree, a large, delicate, empty birdcage. Three small crystal chandeliers. A satin wedding gown. The Regent diamond. A music box, a pillbox, and a snuffbox, all carved and jewelled. A complete moroccan-leather-bound and gold-edged set of Shakespeare. An enormous string of black pearls. A silver carving set, with jade handles. Four sets of diamond-studded andirons and pokers. An Indian inlaid-ivory jewel box.

Not bad duty, I thought. Not a bad way to serve your country. Some poor soldier will be very happy with these. I kept stuffing things into the trunk. I wanted to make someone happy. To do my part.

The heat; my khaki shirt was dripping wet. Thunder. Hurry. I found a large cut-glass fruit bowl and placed it carefully in the trunk. A great pile of stage costumes with "Traviata, Act I" labels attached to them with rusty common pins. Four cylinder Edison records, a dozen thick 78s. One was "Annie Laurie," sung by John McCormack. I didn't read the others. What treasures. A thick velvet-covered footstool. A Louis XV commode. The throne with the Stone of Scone. Two American Colonial corner cupboards. All of Bach's original music scores in seventy-three huge bundles. A forty-room English castle, furnished. The trunk took everything. An old, ornate wood-and-glass hearse. Napoleon and Josephine's bed. Three stuffed owls, a Victorian coach. The Venus de Milo. She was sticking out of the dirt, and I spent a long time carefully digging her up with my entrenching tool. She excited me as I uncovered her, but I had no time. "La Gioconda." I discarded it. Must choose with care. Michelangelo's "Pietà." The original puppet Pinocchio. All the drapes and mirrors from Versailles. And sixty-seven issues of the *Saturday Evening Post* from 1928 and 1929. Riches. I was a conquistador. Ah, a jewelled dagger. I put it in my belt. A sword. I hung that beside the dagger, swashbuckling at my side. A pirate's pistol, loaded. Three rifles, a flamethrower, four hand grenades, two bazookas, a tank, seven napalm bombs.

Let them come, the bastards. I was ready. My

things were heaped high, spilling out of the trunk. I could get anyone—pick them off one by one—anyone who tried to take my things. Mosquitoes buzzed and bit me. Men's shouts in my ears: anguish. *My* stuff. *I* found it. Natural rights—stake a claim. Noise. Scuffles. Machine-gun fire. Snipers? I took out my weapons. I flung hand grenades. Fired the bazookas. Used the flamethrower. Scores of the enemy screamed and fell at my feet. I looked. Tim O'Connell lay there, dead, his face grinning.

It began to rain, making the flamethrower useless. A red thing was coming at me. Fast. The rain was thick and hot, steaming. The red thing ran. I could not see. I took out the pirate's pistol, aimed as best I could, and fired. It went off with a tremendous boom. There were blood flecks on my hand from the powder. The red thing quivered and fell. I looked to my side. My treasure was safe. I eased forward a few steps. The rain was pouring down like hot silver coins, and I slogged ahead in the mud and vines. The form was still. I turned it over quickly with my foot.

It was my son, Charlie, the red thing his umbrella. It stood bottom side up, filling fast with water. Charlie's tiny red mouth was open slightly. I snatched him to me. I was crying, and the rain kept coming. I kissed his limp and weightless body again and again. I carried him to the trunk. I flung out all the stuff. It took me hours. I put Charlie in gently among the cloth flowers, got the umbrella, put that in beside him. I closed the trunk. Slowly, dragging my treasure, in the stupendous jungle rain, I began to try to find my way back.

A Reunion

HAM AND POTATO SALAD, red wine, sliced turkey, plain *pita*, Greek tossed salad and Greek cheese, rice pilaf, cold sliced lamb, French bread, black olives, a cake, *baklavá*, and *courabiédes* cookies were all arranged on the dining-room table, which had been spread with a new white cloth. Tom had even lighted two tall white candles at either side of the bowl of carnations and roses his father had brought home from his flower shop.

The relatives were all in the living room: Tom's father, his two brothers and their wives, his sister and her husband, a fat dark uncle (his father's brother), and three cousins. Most of the men were smoking. Two small nieces dressed in red jumpers ran around squealing. Tom, who had taken three days off from his senior year at college for this occasion, passed time talking with his oldest brother. But he was not aware of what they were saying; he was aware of tension in the crowded room.

In the center of the couch, as if enthroned, sat his mother, the person who was half—more than half—the reason for the excitement. She was about to be reunited with her only sister, Mary, who had arrived from Greece the night before. She sat calmly. She had been dressed in a new wine-colored dress, pale sheer stockings, her good black shoes. Fat white plastic beads ringed her throat and one of her wrists; a tarnished brass bracelet dangled from her other wrist; a big rhinestone pin dragged down the front of her dress. Tom looked at her folded hands, her loose, soft torso, her completely smooth forehead, her black eyes staring ahead of her at nothing in particular, her small listless mouth, and realized that of all the people in the room she was most her usual self—the least concerned, the least involved. He wondered if the reunion meant anything at all to her.

If it meant nothing, that was understandable. She had not seen her sister for thirty-six years—not since her own marriage. She had been fifteen at the time, and Mary had been seven. Immediately after the wedding, she had left Greece with Tom's father for America. They had come to this seaport town in New England where his uncle had known someone, and they had stayed. Life had not been pleasant for either of the sisters. Tom's mother had had four children in quick succession, and one stillbirth. His father, intent only on making a living, had worked long hours in restaurants and flower shops, leaving her alone a lot, neglected. She had almost at the very start sunk into a private, silent world from which she never fully emerged. She always seemed to know what was happening around her, but she made little response to it. Mary had suffered, too. In Greece, the girls' parents had both died in an epidemic, and Mary had spent her childhood being shuffled among relatives. At seventeen, she had impetuously married a worthless man, who soon deserted her and their small son. He had died just a year before, in the bed of his most recent mistress. The son, Alex, was now twenty-three. When he was twenty-one, he had found a way to come to America. For two years, he had washed dishes in a restaurant, saving his money until he had enough to rent a small apartment and send for his mother.

Now she was here. Tom, with his father and brothers, had met her at the railroad station last night. Under the windy shed, she had looked at Tom's pale face and said his mother's name. Then she had hugged him close to her, and wept, and kissed him all over his face, covering it with wetness. At first he was embarrassed at this public display, but then he found himself weeping, too, and unaccountably kissing her just as hard, again and again.

Everyone agreed it would be better to wait one day for the reunion of the sisters. Mary should have a good night's sleep first. Besides, some of the relatives were anxious about the reunion—about the strain and possible sorrow of it. Who knew what the older, lost woman might do? Or the younger, foreign widow? This afternoon, Tom had daydreamed that as soon as they met, his mother would snap out of her long coma. Suddenly she would be lithe and graceful as Tom had been told she once was. She would speak sensibly again, and show his father love and respect—something Tom had never witnessed. Singing, she would scrub the whole house, and cook a marvellous *spanakópita*—a spinach-and-cheese pie made with thin, thin delicate leaves of pastry. She would shed the shabby housedress she insisted on wearing, and put on a good dress, and leave off her frivolous jewelry forever, and go shopping, and— He had shut off the dream with no regrets, since he was used to dreaming, and had gone with his father to the delicatessen to buy the food that waited in the dining room.

Tom went out to look at the kitchen clock. Eight-thirty. They ought to be here; they had said eight. Restless, worried, not knowing what to do with himself, he went upstairs. He slipped into his father's room and turned on the light. Quietly, he slid open a drawer of his father's bureau. From the place where it always lay under clothing, he removed the framed, brownish photograph of his parents' wedding. Before an Oriental tapestry stood his father—dark, tall, proud—in a tuxedo with wide satin lapels. He was sleek and defiant. Beside him stood his bride. She was small and slender. She wore a richly embroidered vest and a long-sleeved white blouse. A score of gold coins, her dowry, glittered on the front of her white bridal headpiece. Her face was light-skinned, full, perfectly symmetrical; her eyes were large and dark. At either side of the couple, attendants stood stiffly in tuxedos. One of them was Tom's uncle; he was not fat here. Tom's grandfather—distinguished, with a mustache—was sitting on a chair in front of the bride. At one end of the group was a tiny dark child in a long dress with a lace collar, staring intently. That was Mary, with her hair in bangs. There was a confused, wistful expression on her face, a slight tilt to her head, as if the festivities of a big sister's marriage were too much to comprehend.

Tom looked at the photograph for a long time, then put it back carefully and went downstairs.

In the living room, his sister touched his arm. She was like her father, tall and bony. "Tom, sit down and take it easy," she said. "Don't worry so much. You know how it'll be. So don't get in a state."

His brothers, his sister were always urging him to relax. He was the youngest. They always said that they took things as their father did, that they saw life as it was—crooked and full of displaced persons, buried emotions, sorrow—accepted it, and went on about their business. They had long since learned to hide scars.

There was a noise in the drive, and Tom went to

the back door. Outside, a taxi had stopped, and his aunt and cousin were hurrying toward the kitchen, their faces white in the moonlight.

"Whew, what a cold climate you have!" Aunt Mary said as she removed a kerchief from her head. She spoke in Greek. She kissed Tom—less intensely this time. His two brothers came out of the living room. More kissing.

"Take off your coats," Tom said in Greek. He tossed the cold, heavy coats onto the railing that led upstairs. Mary looked young and strong. She was slim and dark. Her eyes were the same as his mother's eyes, only brighter. Her nose was the same, too—straight—but thicker. In fact, she looked a lot like his mother, but she did not have her pallor, her basically delicate beauty. And her hair was different. His mother's hair was black, cut to the jawline, and hung straight and shiny. His aunt's was chestnut-colored and dull in the kitchen light, and she wore it gathered in a chignon at the back of her neck, in the European style. She was simply dressed in a plain, black fitted suit with a gold lapel pin, sheer black stockings, black semi-high heels.

Now she nodded, as if to say, "I'm ready," but she stood there wringing her strong hands and frowning. Tom's heart quickened. His brothers grew quiet. Alex said softly, pointing a heavy finger at his mother, "Now, don't forget what I told you. No tears, no crying."

In procession, they marched through the dining room, past a brooding icon on the wall, through the old-fashioned archway, into the living room. Tom stopped near the archway; he was too nervous to sit. His brothers went to their chairs. Alex led Mary to her sister; then he stepped back and sat down.

Everyone had stopped talking. Only the little girls chirped, and their mother was hushing them. Everyone was looking at Tom's mother.

Mary bent down to her sister and embraced her lightly. She kissed her with gentle restraint—once, on the cheek. The kiss made a soft noise.

All around the room the relatives looked as if they might weep, but no one did. The fat dark uncle grunted in a kind of animal sadness.

Mary said, "Do you remember me?"

On the couch, Tom's mother looked at her sister's face, then down at the flowered carpet. The room was still.

Mary said again, "Do you remember me?"

"Of course," Tom's mother said. She spoke with a small, lopsided grin, as if to say, "Do you all think I'm a fool that I don't know who my own sister is?" They had told her that her sister was coming. She had said only, "Really? When?" They had told her, and she had shrugged.

Tom leaned against the archway. He thought that the moment of reunion had been cool and dignified. Proper. Then he wondered, Had it been proper? Wouldn't a tearful outburst have been better—a strong wild embrace, an acknowledgment of mutual suffering?

Alex, darkly handsome, broke the silence with a chuckle, merriness in his brown eyes. He stood up and said, "Aunt, tell her what you told me. Tell her what you said you used to call my mother when she was a little girl."

Tom's mother kept her mouth tightly closed. She looked like a child who needed coaxing to recite.

"Come on, Auntie. Tell her," Alex said.

"Galítsa," Tom's mother said quickly, smirking.

"There," Alex said, triumphant. "Now you *know* she remembers my mother." "*Galítsa*" is a term of endearment, meaning roughly "dark little bird." Alex turned to the roomful of people and said in broken English, "She used to call my mother that because my mother was so black." He snorted and then laughed out loud.

All at once, the relatives burst into laughter and shouts. They stood, lit fresh cigarettes, moved about in nervous relief. The aunt met and kissed everyone and was kissed in turn. Someone started the phonograph, loud, and Greek music filled the rooms. Tom's uncle and his reserved father and Alex talked and gesticulated and drank ouzo together.

Sitting beside her sister, Mary spoke softly, asking small domestic questions about her life. Tom's mother didn't answer. Once, she grabbed Mary's pocketbook and held on to it, challenging her. One of Tom's brothers, short and rugged and dark, tugged it gently out of her hands, saying, "Come on now, Mama, give it back to her. You have your own pocketbook right there. You know better than that. It's not yours." He winked at his aunt, and she winked back.

Tom's mother had a fixation about money. She always carried loose change and bills loaded in the front pockets of her dress as if they were saddlebags. On the few occasions she dressed up, she stuffed it all into a pocketbook and kept it with her. She guarded every penny. No one knew exactly how much she had wheedled from her family or pilfered from pocketbooks and wallets and pants' pockets over the years. No one cared, if it gave her pleasure.

Galítsa had winked back. Tom had seen her. So, that quickly. Beneath whatever pity and love Mary could possibly have felt, there was already collusion—an entering into the tacit, easy collective judgment of the sane. Tom thought, As if my mother doesn't know what's going on. As if she's not indulging in a collusion of her own. But then he thought, Why not wink? He himself was often in on private family jokes about his mother's quirks. Why should his aunt be different?

What did he expect? One had to keep a hold on one's own reality, too.

Now his mother sat unconsciously patting her own pocketbook, appraising her sister, giving her a frank, prolonged once-over.

With a bang, his father put down his shot glass. "Hey, everybody!" he shouted. He was forceful, gay, perhaps a little drunk. A thin film of sweat shimmered on his big forehead. "What are we waiting for? Let's eat!"

Almost everyone jumped up and went toward the dining room. Those nearest the table took up plates and began to devastate the orderly platters of food that Tom and his sister had laid out. The candles' soft yellow flames scudded, the flowers stood vivid and bright. Talking and laughing, the hungry relatives helped one another load their clinking plates and fill their glasses with dark red wine. On the phonograph a clarinet wailed in the high, thin loops of a Greek song.

The sisters did not get up. Left alone, they sat together on the couch, holding hands like little children. From where he stood by himself at the end of a scattered line, Tom watched his mother as she played with her sister's fingers. And then he saw her look longingly into her sister's eyes. Above the din in the other room, above the crying clarinet, he heard his mother say clearly and slowly, "Do you remember me?"

A Day in the Country

THE MORNING SUN woke Jeff Archambault. His wife, Marie, was sleeping beside him in a profusion of long black hair and a sheer pink cotton nightgown. Jeff stared at the Victorian plaster ring of leaves and flowers in the middle of the high ceiling in the big room and tried to remember what was important today. There was something. He got up and dressed. Outside the windows, the river was slate blue and ruffled. The sky was the same color, except for a faint, ominous mauve rim in the east.

Jeff remembered as he was putting a pot of coffee on the stove: Grammie was picking out her coffin today. His maternal grandmother, she was alone in the world except for Jeff and his brothers, Ray and Jack. She lived in a small unit in the housing project for old people, a new cluster of brick buildings that had usurped part of the town green. She had asked Jeff if he would take her on the errand today, and since it was Saturday he could not say no.

When the coffee was percolating, Marie came to the kitchen in her bare feet. She said, "Nine o'clock. You're up early." Her voice was gritty with sleep, her eyes almost closed. Normally, she and Jeff slept late on weekends. They both taught in the borough high school and had to get up very early during the week.

"I have to take Grammie," he said.

"Oh. Yes."

They had some toast, and Marie lit a cigarette. Jeff did not smoke. They sat silent in the room full of light.

"I'll be home early," Jeff said, kissing her at the door.

"Yes, don't forget, sweetheart." She smoothed his rough blond hair. "There's the poetry reading this afternoon at the college."

The Samuel J. Gellhorn Homes of Pequot, Connecticut, was a ten-minute drive away. At one of a long line of identical plywood doors, Jeff rang the bell. His tiny grandmother opened the door. Jeff was six feet tall and had to bend down to kiss her. Her hair was white and silky. Her eyes were blue and clear, like Jeff's. Though she was seventy-eight years old, she did not need glasses. Her skin was brown, mottled, and loose. Her legs were bowed, covered with cotton stockings, and did not taper to visible ankles but ended abruptly, thickly spilling over the tops of small black shoes.

She smiled and said, "Yes, come in and I'll make you a cup of tea." Jeff told her that he had eaten already. Sometimes she was a little deaf—perhaps intentionally. "You must be kind of hungry," she said. She put the teakettle on the stove, and in a few minutes they were seated in the dining alcove with cookies and two cups of steaming tea. The cups were big, ecru-colored, and had red magnolias painted on the sides. Jeff remembered them from childhood. Grammie kept things so well—the furniture and pieces of virtu looked just as they had when he used to visit her when he was little. She had lived six miles from the center of town, in a large white house with plenty of space and grass and trees. His grandfather, Matthew Lemming, had been alive then; he was a railroad engineer, and Jeff did not see much of him. Now his picture stood on the big console Stromberg-Carlson radio, on a crocheted doily hard with starch. A hearty man with white hair and a big hooked nose, he was laughing jovially straight at the camera, straight at you. Twenty years before, he had been killed in an accident near New Haven. In the family, the accident was like a great historical event. Grammie measured life by it: "He joined the Navy three years before the accident." "She was born five months after the accident." That was how she had lived out the past twenty years. That, and eating a piece of liver, a boiled potato, a cup of custard. Taking saccharine in her tea, moving about with a little piece of cloth dabbing at the furniture, at the dust. She mumbled now about the dust. How it was *so* dusty in the middle of town, summer or winter; so noisy and dirty. But you had to pay the price "if you was to be convenient to things"—to the A. & P., to the doctor's office, to the public library, where she read the papers every afternoon, seated stiffly under the portraits of early townsmen.

She stood in her black winter coat and hat and said, "Well, let's go." Outside, when Jeff tried to help her into the car, she waved her freckled hands at him and frowned and struggled by herself, almost falling over backward as she climbed in. "You're so skinny," she said. "Save it for your wife. You young people are helpless today. Don't get enough exercise."

Jeff tried not to laugh. "Where to?" he asked her.

"Why, the church," she said, and she looked irritated.

"The *church?*"

"Just do as I say."

Jeff drove west on the old potholed tar highway. Grammie still went to the Pentecostal Tabernacle where she had been married and where, to please his dying mother, Jeff himself had married two years before. Moving now past granite boulders and cedar trees on bleak, yellow-stubble fields, he hoped that Grammie had not become suddenly senile.

At the church—a sagging, peeling white-painted wooden building with a small bell tower—he found over a dozen cars parked in the frozen mud lot. "Seems to be *some*thing going on," he said.

"Course there is," Grammie said.

Jeff went around to help her out of the car. Her claw of a hand hooked onto his own large hand, and when she was standing at last, she let go and made a loose fist and waved him off furiously.

An icy wind whipped at them as they went up three stone steps into the church. Forward, through open doors, there was a roseate silence among the empty pews; the sound of voices came from downstairs. Jeff and Grammie descended slowly. In the basement hall, about forty people had gathered. Along a whitewashed wall of the big room stood a long row of coffins on sawhorse stands. The upper half of each coffin was open, and large cards with writing were propped on the closed halves. Across the room, people clustered beside a table spread with a white cloth and set with a large punch bowl and plates of cookies. They stood with glasses of raspberry-colored liquid in their hands, talking and laughing. A few people were examining the coffins— bending down close for a good look and running their hands along the wood and reading the cards, murmuring.

Jeff said, "Jesus. What's all this?"

Grammie smiled brightly and said, "The Reverend thought it up. For the church building fund. Don't you think it's clever?"

Jeff could see the young minister across the room talking with an old woman. Tall, with fine, thinning blond hair and a narrow long nose, he was new in the parish. He wore clear-plastic-rimmed glasses. He nodded at Jeff, and Jeff nodded back. They had never seen each other before.

A thin, stooped man came up to Grammie. "Hi, Ethel," he said. "Glad to see you could make it."

"Hello, Conrad. You know my grandson?"

"Sure. One of Mildred's boys. Rest her soul. How you doing, son?"

Jeff shrugged, and then he smiled to be polite. "What's going on?" he asked.

"It's the Reverend's idea," Conrad answered. "Him and some of the other young fellows in the parish built these here things, and whoever wants can buy their own coffin cheap, and do the church a big help, too. Funeral people are robbers anyway. Just look at some of the prices here, and you'll see what I mean. Does your heart good. I'm thinking of getting one myself."

They went down the line. There were twelve coffins, all made of pine but stained in various wood colors—cherry, maple, oak, mahogany. They seemed well constructed: smooth edges, good joints, fine finish, precisely spaced shiny brass or stainless-steel handles. The cards told who had made them, what they were made of, and how much they cost. The prices ran from seventy-five to two hundred dollars.

Grammie shuffled along, intent, wagging. Finally she stopped. "This one," she said. "I don't need to look an inch more. This is perfect. He'd have loved it."

She was standing before a small casket that was stained mahogany. It had finely bevelled edges. The hinges were brass; the handles, too. The lid was rubbed to a high gloss, and it had an overlapping Moorish-looking scroll carved all around the border about two inches in from the edge. The inside was lined with rose-colored satin, and there was a matching pillow with a white lace edge. Jeff read the card: "James Pickering; interior by Mrs. Pickering; pine, stained mahogany, 65", satin lined and polyurethane foam filled; price: $189.50."

"Why, that's a steal," Grammie said, reading the price out loud to Jeff. "And look. It won first prize." There was a blue ribbon stuck to the bottom of the card. "Well, that was easy. Is James Pickering here? And where do you pay?" She looked relieved.

Conrad said, "Right down the end of the line. Go ahead, Ethel. You're the first to buy. Good for you. Now maybe it'll loosen some of the others up. Why, Mabel Evans said it's heathen, and I know darn well it isn't. *She* may be. The good Lord knows what He's doing, and works in mysterious ways." He loped toward the minister's group as Jeff and Grammie moved on.

Grammie said, "The good Lord my foot." She smiled. She knew that Jeff was an atheist. A few years ago, she had announced that she was, too. She went to church functions to pass the time away, she said.

At the end of the line, a card table had been set up, and a green cash box lay open on it. Two women sat behind the table; one was fat, the other thin.

"Hi, girls," Grammie said. "I want to pay for the one in the middle. The blue ribbon. What's his name?"

Jeff said, "James Pickering."

"Yes. Is he here?"

The fat woman said, "No. Besides the Reverend, there ain't no young people here, except him." She pointed at Jeff.

Grammie said, "Well, you tell Mr. Pickering for me that that's an awful good job he did, and I appreciate it. Now, let me pay you. And I don't have room in that place they've stuck me—you'll store it in the church somewhere till I need it, is that correct?"

"That's correct, Mrs. Lemming," the fat woman said.

Grammie fumbled in her black pocketbook. Finally, she came up with a pale-blue rayon change purse; it was bulging. She unzipped it and took out a pack of bills, opened them, wet her fingers on her tongue, and began to count twenties. She laid ten of them on the table. Jeff was surprised. She had no income—the big house had been consumed in mortgages. She must have been saving out of her Social Security for a long time.

The thin woman said, "Now, Ethel, you don't have to pay cash, you know. Just one-third down."

Grammie laughed. "Give me a receipt, please," she said.

The thin woman wrote it out slowly in a good Palmer script. "There," she said, handing it across the table with a half-dollar coin and a ten-dollar bill. "Thanks, Ethel. God bless you."

Grammie took the receipt, looked at it, folded it once, put it in her pocketbook, and turned away. Some people nearby were staring at her, silent. "You'd think they never saw an old lady before," she said.

The minister came over, and he smiled in a fishy way and said, "We want to thank you for your help, Mrs. Lemming." He looked uncomfortable.

"It's nothing," Grammie said. "But you tell Mr. Pickering what a nice job he did, and I sure like it. Must be related somehow to Selma Pickering. You know him, Jeffery?"

"No."

138

"Well, let's go."

"Won't you have some punch?" the minister said.

"What?" Grammie said.

The minister repeated the question, smiling at Jeff.

Grammie said, "I thought you were offering to punch me. No. No, thank you. Too sweet. I never could tolerate it. Or punch parties, neither." She started marching down beside the line of coffins.

A tall, heavy man was examining one carefully. "I think I like this one," he said loudly to a small woman beside him. "I think I do."

"Get it, Todd," Grammie said. "Get it."

He looked surprised, intruded upon.

A bit farther, Grammie stopped and barely touched the James Pickering coffin. "Grand," she said, and sighed and walked on.

When they got outside, Grammie shivered violently. The wind was shifting. Gray clouds were drifting in above thin trees that surrounded the church. Their dark fine branches knocked together. "It's getting around to the northeast," Grammie said. "I could tell by my legs. We'll have some snow before tomorrow." She turned and looked up at the belfry. Her eyes glazed, strands of her white hair blew back. Her breath caught, and she said, "Matthew. I'm ready now."

At two o'clock that afternoon, Jeff and Marie were seated together in the Ogilvie Room upstairs in the Ogilvie Library at Ogilvie College for Women. The room was painted beige, its two square supporting columns orange. There were big white oilpaper globes on the overhead lights. Rare books were locked up in glass cases around the walls. An Oriental carpet almost covered the floor. Ahead of Jeff was a small, deep well window. The room was high above the ground, and through small panes he could see only the heavy gray sky.

Marie was holding Jeff's hand. Her hand was small and slightly moist; the fingernails were long and white. Her arms were slender and had a touch of pale-brown hair on them. She was wearing a pink wool dress, black patent-leather shoes. Her legs were slim, elegant. Her nose was nice. Small, but not pert. Strong. Her wonderful brown eyes . . .

"Jeff," she whispered, "you're staring at me."

He looked down at the blood-red sweater his grandmother had knitted for him.

After a while, Marie said, "Don't be depressed."

"About what?"

"You know. Grammie."

"I wasn't. But you know, at the time I thought it was funny."

The room was filling, everyone settling into rows of metal folding chairs—several members of the faculty, a dozen bright-faced girls, a few stray college boys, a group of creaking alumnae in long dark dresses. There must have been thirty people—not bad for a Saturday. Why hold it on a Saturday, anyway? Usually the college poetry readings were held Sunday afternoons. This poet must have a tight circuit—probably reading at another New England college tomorrow. Jeff had wanted to be a poet once. For a long time he had written verses. But after three years of sending them out to the little magazines and getting them back, he had given up. He still kept the poems at home in a brown folder in his desk, though, with his name and address typed on each of them.

"Here comes Mr. Revere," Marie said. He was head of the English department. Marie had gone to

Ogilvie College; Jeff had met her there, in the library reference room.

"And here's Mallory behind him," Jeff said.

The two men went to the podium together. Mr. Mallory sat beside the table. The members of the audience cleared their throats and coughed. When it grew quiet, Mr. Revere, who was about sixty, cleared *his* throat and said some soft, witty words of introduction. And then, smiling, he said, "Without further ado, I give you Mr. Mallory. Tom?"

The audience applauded gently. Tom Mallory got up and replaced Mr. Revere at the lectern. He was a very tall, very handsome man in his middle thirties—an almost perfect romantic image of a poet. He was wearing a Glen-plaid jacket, a gray shirt, and a maroon ascot. He had a mass of light brown curly hair, pale blue eyes, wind-burned skin that was flushed, probably from the wine that poets and lecturers were reputedly given at the customary faculty luncheon. When he spoke, his voice was light, rather raspy. He sounded and looked like a large, strong, intelligent eighteen-year-old boy.

He read a dozen short poems, stopping to say something of the background of each. He used a lot of first-person pronouns. "My problem here. . . ." "When I was about eleven. . . ." "My belief. . . ." "On my farm. . . ." "I like to think. . . ." "It seems to me that the Depression wasn't really mine." Every time he uttered a curse word in his poems, or a frank anatomical one, his two children, who were sitting up front with his surprisingly homely wife, giggled and looked at each other. They were beautiful children—a boy and a girl under ten years of age with long blond hair.

After reading all the short poems, Mallory paused, poured some water from a pitcher on the table, and gulped it down. Everyone squirmed and changed folded legs and cleared throats again. Then, to finish the session, Mallory read a very long prose poem about his grandfather's dying. He read it fast, so fast it hurt the ears to try to listen. The voice went on and on.

Jeff could not hear much of it. He stared at the gray patch of window. Occasionally, he watched Mallory's full pink mouth moving quickly, unceasing, with spittle at its corners. He heard: ". . . in the bare attic room, the rain and the wind as thin as a witch . . . his white hair and sagging flesh . . . I, afraid beneath the eaves' raw wood . . . his apple face and promiscuity . . . the sleigh and hauled the yule log in . . . she gave him sons . . . this drunk, roaring Lear raged and cursed and called her whore . . . with her apron wiped her eyes . . . caressed her thick black tresses . . . jokes of peckers, humping sheep . . . and taught me to be gentle . . . screamed, refused to die, they held him down . . . gave her bonbons and his hot strength and lunged . . . like a Sisyphus with our New England stone . . . struggled, knocked the basin over, slopping all the green wallpaper roses . . . that last fall with baths of alcohol . . . mosquitoes, swore he'd patch the screen . . . she swabbed him, kept her vigil . . . canning her preserves, the smell of kerosene . . . open family Bible with its dark pressed flowers . . . how could one believe that those strong hands . . . what we all are coming to . . . rattling crash his breath was gone . . . what does not wither but the stones? . . . her white hands trembling on her face . . . then they took the sheet and covered up his head."

Mr. Mallory closed his book and left the lectern. There was a moment of silence, and then the audience clapped strongly for a long time. He got up and bowed from the waist, and his lips formed the silent words "Thank you." Everyone filed slowly out of the room. Descending the two winding, long flights of marble stairs, Marie and Jeff passed a large brass chandelier, a bust of Shakespeare in a niche, and Colonial portraits of the college founder's ancestors. They went out into the cold. The clouds were low, a thick gray blanket now. Surely it would snow.

Back at the apartment, Jeff made drinks, and they both got a little drunk and ate dinner.

"Did you like Mallory?" she said.

"Some of it. You?"

"No. I couldn't understand, he read so fast."

"I kind of liked the grandfather, himself, what *I* could get. He reminded me of my own grandfather, Matthew. What little I remember of him."

Jeff thought of Grammie. Marie got up from the table, weaving, and went to his chair and kissed him. They went to bed and made love and fell asleep curled together some time before eight o'clock.

Jeff awoke and looked at the luminous dial of the clock on the bureau: it was seventeen minutes before ten. He got up and put on his clothes. "Marie," he said. She did not answer. He went to a window. It was snowing—small white flakes under the streetlight. Starting fine like that, it would be a big storm. A thin coat of snow already lay in spots on the black road. The lights of the factory across the river were invisible. The world was a secret, manifest only in a small ring of white light. "Marie," Jeff said. She stirred. "It's snowing. It's beautiful. Look." She got up on one elbow and looked out the window next to her. "Mm," she said, and lay down again.

"A dream," he said. And after a moment, "I'm kind of hungry. Are you?"

"Maybe."

"I'll go to Ray's for a pizza. I'll bring it home and we can eat it together and watch an old movie on TV."

Marie said nothing. She liked to sleep almost better than anything else. Jeff did not; he considered it a waste of time, an unfortunate necessity. All that silence, inactivity, when you could at least be reading. But Marie could sleep anytime. She was lucky, in a way. Jeff was surprised that he had just dozed here with her. He must have been very tired. Probably the liquor. He did not remember any dreams. Now he wanted to escape from this emptiness, this sleep.

"O.K. then," he said. "I'm going to Ray's. You'll get up and make a fresh pot of coffee. Right?"

"Yes, yes," she said, sounding irritated.

He left the house and drove slowly through the center of the little town. It was quiet, with few people about. The red neon lights were beautiful in the falling snow. The housing project for old people lay in darkness. They were all asleep. Jeff drove to the edge of town, out by the quarry. On the highway leading north, huddled together, were a small, dimly lit Quonset-hut bar, a closed, darkened grocery store, and his brother Ray's place—the Crescent Pizza Palace. Jeff pulled up in the asphalt drive. The snow looked black as it fell in swift patches before the bright, steamy plate-glass windows. Inside, a friend of Ray's stood on a stepladder. He was painting the woodwork a dark-cream color. He laughed and kidded Ray. Five teen-age boys were stuffed into a booth, eating grinders. They were laughing, too, and lifting Cokes to their mouths between bites. Another customer, a middle-aged man, stood by the cash register.

Jeff's brother Ray was taking a pizza out of the big streamlined black oven on its stilted chrome legs. He used a flat wooden shovel with a long handle to transfer the bubbling pizza to a counter. He was a short, strong man in his early thirties, and he knew what he was doing. He rimmed the hot pizza out of its pan with a spatula and placed it on a board, cut it swiftly and deftly in wedges, slipped it between paper plates, put it into a bag, and handed it to the waiting customer. "Ninety," Ray said, closing his heavy-lidded eyes and opening them slowly. He was shy, quiet. When the man had gone, Ray said, "What's new?"

"Nothing. I felt kind of hungry and came for a pizza."

"Where's Marie?"

"Home. She fell asleep. Quiet tonight, huh?"

"Yeah. I think I'll close early. Before it gets too slippery out. I'm going to listen to the fight first." He turned and looked at the clock. It was five past ten. "It should start any time," Ray said, and he went to the marble-top table that he used for cutting dough. He turned up the volume on a crackling transistor radio. The fight evidently had not started yet, and the announcer was discussing the odds, the fighters' merits and weaknesses. His voice filled the restaurant. It was nasal, almost incomprehensible.

Jeff did not care for the fights. If there was one on the radio or TV in a room where he had to be, he would listen or watch listlessly. After a while, though, it became mesmerizing.

One of the teen-agers yelled, "Hey, Ray, let's form a pool!" Everyone agreed, cheering, even the fellow on the ladder. Ray made out the bet slips, and put them into a big saucepan. The pool was half a dollar a head. He came to Jeff and said, "You in?"

"I don't think so."

"Why not?"

"I don't know. I don't really like the fights." He wanted to say, "I don't approve of two guys beating the hell out of each other in front of a mob, for money or not."

"Come on," said the painter, a short, bald fat man. "Help the pot."

"Yeah, yeah!" the teen-agers shouted. Jeff put two quarters on the counter and drew. The torn piece of paper said "6." A good draw, everyone said. A knockout in the sixth was very possible.

Jeff's younger brother Jack walked in. "What the hell is this snow?" he said, stomping down the open center of the restaurant. "Who needs it?" He was twenty-five, five years younger than Jeff. Tall, thin, good-looking, he was a bachelor who never stopped. He was very popular with the girls. A week ago, he had moved out of his father's house to an apartment so that he could have a place to entertain them. Ray did not approve of his leaving their father alone in an empty house. But Jack was young; he had to have his own life, sow his wild oats, get it out of his system before settling down.

"You're just in time," Ray said. "We're picking for the fight. Here. Half a buck."

"What?" Jack raised his arms in a gesture of helplessness and picked Round 11. He paid Ray. There were six pieces of paper left in the pot. Ray offered them. Three teen-agers bought, and Ray and the painter absorbed the rest, dropping their coins into the pot.

One of the teen-agers finished eating, got up. Sometimes he helped in the place. "You want me to mop tonight, Ray?" he said.

"Yeah, Dave, might as well start now. There's no business. I'm closing soon as the fight's over. Sweep first, O.K.? I'll give you an extra buck."

On the radio there was a clanging bell, a buzzing silence, the Brooklynese accents of the ring announcer bellowing names and measurements, rules, the exhortation to shake hands and fight a clean fight.

It began. David was sweeping. The painter was painting. The teen-agers rose from the booth, leaving a tabletop full of used napkins, paper plates, soda bottles, tomato sauce. They lay against the counter, listening intently. "Good," one said. "Yeah. Give it to him. I'm gonna win. This is my round."

David swept in short, steady strokes. Nervous, Jeff went over and cleaned off the table, carefully picking up oily bits of lettuce.

The bell sounded on the radio. End of Round 2. Disappointed groans came from the bald painter. "But I still got it in the ninth," he said. "He'll knock him out in the ninth."

"Naah," one of the long-haired teen-agers said. "He'll take him in the seventh. I got half a buck says so."

The painter laughed out loud, all his big white teeth showing. Placing the brush carefully across the paint can, he lit a long greenish cigar.

Jeff held the moment: the lounging teen-agers, the sweeping boy, his brother Ray in a white apron, his brother Jack looking alert with his black coat still buttoned, the laughing cigar-smoking painter, the bright lights, the shouting radio announcer; outside, the snow, and secretly, inside a nest far away, Marie, asleep. The moment meant a lot, and yet Jeff knew that it meant nothing.

The announcer was shouting, ". . . a left jab, then another right, oh! a left, Cody dancing, faking, Brill taking the punches easy, Cody with a light jab, misses. . . . Cody faking, still dancing, he is beautiful, in beautiful shape, now Brill moving in with a left, grazes Cody's shoulder, oh! a hard right from Brill, Cody moving back, and there's the bell, end of Round 5."

David, a quiet high-school boy who was getting A in Russian and F in history, set down the mop and pailful of sudsy water. He began to swab the asphalt-tile floor.

Jeff squeezed the bridge of his nose with his

thumb and forefinger and closed his eyes. It was his round. "Cody has opened a cut over Brill's right eye, blood pouring out of it. . . . Brill shoots a left blindly, misses, Cody in there, a right, then a left to the chest, left, left to Brill's ear, Brill moving away—he looks in bad shape, he moves in, swings a wild right at Cody's head, Cody ducks, a big punch. . . . Cody in there with a left hook, misses, a quick jab to the bleeding cut, Brill holding his right up to it—a big, powerful man this Brill, and make no mistake about it, he's hurt, but not afraid. . . . Oh! a wicked left by Cody on the right side of Brill's head. . . . There's the end of the sixth, and this could be the telling round."

Jeff kept his eyes closed. He wished it had ended in the first with a knockout. It should be called, for God's sake.

Seventh round. Eighth. Tenth. The cut opening wider. Brill's other eye injured now, too, and puffing up fast. A lot of clinches. Brill down on one knee, up at the count of five. Twelfth round. The bright lights in the restaurant. The poet reading. Grammie choosing easily— a Moorish scroll carved on its lid. Marie asleep, no one to wake her. Perhaps. A man destroying another, and millions of people across the land hunched in the snowy night, listening beside radios, watching in closed-circuit-TV movie theatres, tuned in, the fight beamed halfway across the world by satellite.

Fourteenth round. Cody is asking Brill something. Cody is shouting, drumming in punches at his leisure now. Why don't they stop it? Brill is slogging, swinging wide. His face ruined. One eye still bleeding, the other swollen almost shut. David has stopped mopping, is standing beside the radio, leaning on the mop handle. There is murder in his eyes, sweat on his freckled forehead from lifting the heavy wet gray mop. Or from his part in the fight? A gentle boy. Surely. His father ran away, disappeared when David was seven; his mother is a whore. He does not know what he will become. He may hitchhike out to California this summer. He is gripping the mop tight. He grits his chipped yellow teeth together and says, "Yes. Yes. Yeah, man, kill him. Kill the son of a bitch. Beat him to a pulp." His eyes have tears standing in them.

The fight went the full fifteen rounds. The judges' decisions were 13–2; 12–2–1; 14–1. Cody easily retained his crown as heavyweight champion of the world.

Ray won the pool. He had picked the fifteenth round the second time he passed the pot.

Jeff said, "Hey, Ray, throw me in a plain pizza, will you?" Ray did. David mopped slowly, making small agonized grunts. The teen-agers played the jukebox. Jack filled Jeff in on his sex life. "Hey, you want to see my new apartment?" he said.

"I don't think so. I'm taking home a pizza—it'll get cold."

"Just for a minute. It's on your way. Cove Street. Come on. Just a quick look."

"All right. Just for a minute."

When the pizza was done, Ray cut it and put it in a bag. Jeff offered to pay, and Ray refused the money. Jeff rang it up himself. Ray wasn't rich.

"The apartment's no great thing," Jack was saying. "But it's mine, a place to do what I want. You know?"

"Sure. Hey, Ray, has Dad been in?" Jeff said.

"He was here earlier tonight."

"How is he?"

"Same. Knees are raising hell, he said, in this weather."

"Same as Grammie," Jeff said. He was going to

tell Ray about her choosing a casket, but there were too many people around. He'd tell him tomorrow. "Good night, Ray."

"O.K., Jeff. Say hello to Marie."

On the way to Cove Street, driving carefully in the rushing snow, Jeff thought about Brill stumbling around in the ring, not giving up.

He parked behind Jack's car on the quiet residential street. There was already over an inch of snow on the ground and the wind was blowing hard from the east, off the river. They went into a big white apartment house with arborvitae out front, and climbed three flights of stairs. The house was old. The stairs creaked, even though they were carpeted. The radiators in the halls whistled and spluttered. A dead smell of past-cooked meals hung in the air.

Jack unlocked one of three doors on the top floor and made a grand-entrance gesture. Jeff went in. The apartment was stifling, with low ceilings and eaves dropping quickly on all sides. It was long and narrow and dark. The first little room was the living room, then came a kitchen and a bedroom. The large sagging double bed just fit. A microscopic bathroom opened off the kitchen. The furniture in all the rooms was battered, misshapen, ugly—a heavy, dirty overstuffed chair, a maple platform rocker, a plywood coffee table with a glass top that had a crack in it. There was an odor of old shoes, of unclean rugs.

My brother, Jeff thought. He said, "How much a month?"

Jack stood beside him, smoking, trying to smile. "Sixty."

"Everything included?"

"Yup."

"You'd rather live here than home?"

"Yup."

"I guess some people like to suffer."

"I'm not suffering. You should see the banana I had up here last night. I couldn't keep her away."

Jeff stared through to the back. He looked at his brother. Standing by the cracked coffee table in this dingy place, Jack suddenly had the melancholy, frightening look of mortality printed on him—in his health, with strong shoulders, ruddy skin, a lean body, big feet, hands in his pockets. With his youth and a whole future life ahead of him, in this place he looked frail and gaunt and dying. And Jeff thought, I look that way, too. He shook his head.

"I told you it was nothing great," Jack said.

"You've got courage."

Jack shrugged.

Jeff said, "I'd better go. The pizza must be like ice by now. And the roads are slippery as hell already. The snow is beautiful, though, isn't it?"

Jack nodded.

"Well, good night." Jeff took a last look. "It's not so bad," he said, "I suppose. If you get a girl in it and a couple of drinks and some music on the stereo."

"No, it's not bad at all. Honest to God. Come over some time. Bring Marie."

"Sure. Well, I'll see you down Ray's."

"Yeah. See you."

The door shut behind him, and Jeff felt as if he were floating down all the stairs in the dim halls.

On the way home, in the snow, he saw the bleeding prizefighter moving blindly in his satin trunks. And he saw Grammie smiling over the James Pickering casket, the handsome poet reading fast, Marie asleep, and now Jack stumbling about in his gloomy small apartment.

He parked the car and took the cold pizza with him. He stood under the streetlight in the dazzling snow. He could see only the small brown house directly across the street on the river bank. The foghorns were sounding faintly out in the bay. The lights in his apartment upstairs in the big Victorian house were all out. After a long time, he held the bagged pizza up before him and let it fall. It made a soft, muffled noise when it landed flat in the snow.

Jeff went upstairs. He tiptoed into the bedroom. The shades were up. There were four large windows. With the street light and the intense whiteness outside, it was almost like twilight in the room. His coat still on, he sat on the bed next to Marie. She moved in her sleep and whimpered. He took her hand. He remembered making love with her early tonight. It seemed a long time ago, unreal. With his free hand, he touched the top of his head. The snow had melted and his hair was wet.

"Marie," he said. "Do you want a glass of milk?"

She did not answer.

He spoke again. "Marie, do you want anything?"

She turned her face away. How she loved to sleep. If only he did. He must learn to, must force himself.

"Marie," he said, bending over her. "Do you love me?"

"Mm."

"Say it. Say you love me."

"Lum y'."

He kissed her hair. It smelled like cigarette smoke and shampoo. A wonderful odor.

He sat in the dark looking out the window at the snow. The words came to his mind, "Matthew, I'm ready now." He squeezed Marie's hand. He felt a weak response. He must not think of this long day any more.

He must undress and get right in beside Marie and go to sleep.

The words came to him again—"I'm ready now" —but he refused to say them.